The 8th Grave

by Ron Hinnenkamp

This book is dedicated to my family.

1

Emily Vandenburg left Minnesota as soon as she graduated from high school in St. Cloud. She set her sights on bigger and better things that did not include life in Central Minnesota, especially its winters. Emily had excelled as a soloist in the choir and been a member of the golf team. Her first stop was Nashville for an attempt at stardom as a country artist. After working in a small craft store for a year without even an audition, she moved on to Branson, Missouri.

Emily worked as a waitress for just over two weeks when she was able to land a part in the Presley Family Shows. Though a backup singer, she felt she was on the way.

Emily loved walking, and frequently walked home after her performances which ended at ten nightly. Starting the second week, she had a sensation of being followed, but did not see anything out of the ordinary. Most of the way back to her apartment she walked along a busy street, full of people leaving the entertainment center of town. The last three blocks were around, or through, a small city park.

She had just finished her third week in the show and was looking forward to the weekend of matinees, leaving her with the evenings free. It was a cool Thursday night, dark because of the cloud cover. Just as she was about to leave the park, she was pulled down from behind and a rag was forced over her face. She fought briefly, but the chemicals in the rag soon turned everything to black.

Emily woke with a throbbing headache and soon realized she was tied hand and foot, and had tape over her mouth.   She was also blindfolded and had no idea of the time of day, nor how long it had been since she had been abducted. She was confined and in some sort of vehicle as she sensed movement.

Emily had not been in Branson long enough to make friends. Who would miss her? Would they just assume she had left town? She started to panic and tried to scream, but no sound came through the tape.

Emily awoke to a dark shape leaning over her. The nightmare was real. She felt a stinging sensation in her arm and again blacked out.   She awoke as she was being carried through a forest, the sound of snapping twigs were ominous in her panic.

It was cooler now, Emily wondered if it was nighttime. After what seemed like hours, she was dropped unceremoniously on the ground. She felt her arms and legs being tied to the earth. Then, footsteps receding into the distance. Her relief quickly turned to fear as she realized she was alone.

When Emily didn't appear for her Saturday matinee a call was made to her cell, to no avail. Reggie, the show manager, asked around if anyone had seen Emily. Nobody had heard from her since Thursday, and nobody knew where she lived. "I really thought she was more responsible than that," said Reggie. No one thought to call the police.

Saturdays were his day to do his own thing. Often that meant wandering the state land in North Central Minnesota. This warm April Saturday would start a chain of events which eventually would change his habits, in reality his life, forever.

Greg Ireland had graduated from St. Cloud State University three years earlier with a degree in biology led to job offers throughout the area. Unfortunately, most were in fast food and manufacturing. His current job was in telemarketing, providing the opportunity to make new friends in all parts of the country. He had even learned novel ways of ending phone conversations.

He wrestled varsity in high school, with the sport only being Greg's passion because he couldn't handle going left in basketball. Though almost six feet tall and reasonably muscular, lacking any moves going left and managing only a fifteen inch vertical meant he was bench material for the Hornet basketball team. Wrestling had provided school letters in his junior and senior years of high school. He even made it to the section semifinals in his senior year.

Some Saturdays Greg would have his friend Nick Dekich along on his hikes. But Nick liked to sleep in, and Greg was in no mood to wait until noon or later to get going. Nick hauled specialty items throughout the upper Midwest and, to him, sleeping in his own bed was a precious commodity.

State land was not hard to find in this part of Minnesota. You just parked your car and wandered off. About five times a year people got lost just this way. Greg never had a problem as he was accustomed to hiking and knew the signs to find his way. He actually preferred to hike alone.

This week Greg chose the Beaver Falls Land Management Area as his "place to think". At Beaver Falls you could hike all day without reaching the other side near Menahga and State Highway 71. After hiking through a pine forest planted in the 1950s, Greg came upon an open area of about 100 acres. These open areas were plentiful in the northern half of Minnesota as forests and lowlands covered 80 percent of the land.

At first it sounded like a hawk or an eagle as Greg moved on across the open area. A minute later he heard it again. This time it sounded somewhat human. He stood in place, listening. Nothing. As he reached the far side of the opening he heard it again, though much fainter. Again he stopped and listened. Five minutes. Nothing.

There was a time when Greg feared a lot of things. He remembered the time when he was a fifth grader. He came home from school and heard a noise in the basement. He loaded the rifle and slowly went down the stairs to . . . nothing.   Probably just a creak in the old farmhouse.   That was the first time he recognized in himself the trait of going to the problem rather than retreating.

Greg circled the open area trying to locate the source of the noise without success. He was about to continue his hike when he saw a flattened area of tall grass about ten feet in diameter. At the edge of matted area was what looked to Greg like blood splatters.

Greg had little time for poachers. He would call the DNR when he got back to his pickup as cell phone coverage here was poor in the best of conditions.

Figuring the deer was just wounded and suffering, Greg followed the trail of matted grass toward the wood line about fifty yards distant. At the wood line Greg found what would change his thinking about a poacher. Along with a couple of short pieces of rope was a pile of clothing, and a little more blood. He quickly looked around and saw nothing. He looked at his cell phone---no coverage.   Again he looked around and saw nothing.

It was at least a mile back to his truck. Greg made it in less than half the time it took him to get to the meadow.

Bill Haley had worked for the Pike County Sheriff's Department for nearly 12 years and had moved up to chief deputy. He had no aspirations to move beyond that level. Let the sheriff deal with the commissioners and the media – that was not for him. The sheriff, Collin Rafferty, was a political animal. He preferred to spend time in the office and at meetings, leaving the coordination of the department to Haley.

Haley had graduated from Brainerd High School and received his law enforcement training at Alexandria Technical College. From there connections got him the job with the sheriff's office, and the rest was history. Over the years he had taken training in any area the sheriff would fund. Along with forensics and ID theft training, he had spent time at the FBI academy and worked with the state Bureau of Criminal Apprehension.

Haley took Greg's call and met him out on county road 109. The walk back in to the area Greg had seen took a while with Haley asking questions along the way. When they reached the area where Greg had found the blood, Haley circled the area thinking this looked like a rest area for a wounded deer. Just in case, he took a sample of the blood for testing.

They moved on to the spot where Greg had found the rope and clothing . . . nothing. It had to be the spot. It was obvious that someone or something had been there as the grass was bent in several places. In a couple of spots they found the ground dug up. They looked around the immediate area . . . nothing. It was impossible to track in the pine needle covered ground. As they were about to give up, Haley found an earring hanging on a small bush. It was a strange place to find an earring, and they widened their search to about five hundred feet in all directions. Finally, concluding that this was much ado about nothing, they headed back to their vehicles.

Haley didn't doubt what Greg had seen, just figuring it might have been a poacher leaving some clothes behind as he got too warm trailing a wounded animal. He perhaps had returned to collect his clothing while Greg waited for Bill to come out to investigate. Greg jokingly said, "Maybe it was a couple out checking off another county in the '87 Club'". Most outstate people knew about the "naturists" club, with its goal to have sex outdoors in each of the counties in Minnesota. He knew people who claimed to have passed fifty on the list.

Haley was at his desk working on the dreaded paperwork that had become such a big part of law enforcement. The ringing phone was a welcome distraction. "Deputy Haley," he responded and was greeted by Eunice Daggett. Eunice called about once a week with something, "for the department to check on" in her words. "Hello Deputy Haley," Eunice started. "I saw a sheriff's car up on 109 past my place the other day. Were you checking the big truck that was stopped up the road from my place the other night?" Haley, hoping to get out of the office early today asked, "What big truck?" "It was white with no company name on the trailer, and I couldn't see the cab to see if there was a name on it." He told her to let him know if she saw it again and hung up.

Dan Rutledge played college baseball at North Dakota State in Fargo while getting his degree in education. He taught a few years in nearby Hawley while getting his administrative degree. After four years as principal in a small town in South Dakota, he came back to Minnesota. He spent the next thirty years as a principal at Stearns County West, in a town about a half hour from St. Cloud. Now retired, he spent his time golfing and working part time at the golf course.

Looking back at his career, Dan did not know if he had made much of a difference. He had a few problems with students and parents, but mainly it was a job for him. He had looked forward to retiring for several years before the time actually arrived.

With the arrival of April he started

thinking of his trip back to Minnesota after spending the winter in Texas. This was his third year spending the cold months near Houston. Being single, he had been divorced for over ten years, Dan could come and go as he pleased. Packing was minimal, clothing and golf clubs would suffice. As he always said, "For everything else there is MasterCard".

Dan liked to travel on weekends, avoiding rush hour in any big city he happened to travel through. He left Texas, as he had the past couple of years, on the last Saturday of the month. The golf courses would be open by the time he returned to Minnesota.

His stopped the first night at a hotel outside of Kansas City. After dinner at Denny's, he walked across the lot back to his hotel. Just as he stopped at his car to pick up his overnight bag, he felt a terrible jolt in his chest. He vaguely was aware of someone leaning over him and putting something over his face. He awoke to darkness, handcuffed and blindfolded, with no idea where he was. His only sensation was of being in a moving vehicle.

The vehicle stopped and he was pulled out and dropped on the ground. The temperature had dropped since his walk out of Denny's. The person who had abducted him was strong as he picked up Dan and carried him for a long time before dropping him on the ground. He felt a chain wrapped around the handcuffs, then heard the click of a lock being closed. He heard the sound of the abductor walking away and, left with only the silence of the forest, Dan felt fear taking over. What had he done to deserve this, and what was next? The tape over his mouth prevented him from calling out.

"Hey Haley, phone for you," yelled Cliff Devlin, the department dispatcher early on the day after Easter. It was Eunice calling with her weekly report.
 "That white truck was back again day before yesterday, got there at noon and stayed until after dark." Haley asked Eunice if she had seen anyone around the truck. She told him that it was there when she got home from the dollar store after getting candy for the grandchildren, and was still there when it got dark. It was not there in the morning when she let her dog out.

Haley was about to drive out to check the area, mainly to let Eunice know that the department was on the job. But a multi-car accident call out on Highway 10 diverted his attention and Eunice was forgotten.

April Stevenson was an outgoing, attractive blond who took pride in keeping herself in shape. When she was home at her apartment in Milwaukee, she kept a regular schedule at Anytime Fitness down the block. When her career took her on the road, she would put in her miles running outside if no workout facility was nearby.

April traveled the throughout the upper Midwest as writer for Midwest Travel magazine. She started with the magazine after graduation from the University of Wisconsin just over five years before. She loved the freedom of setting her own schedule.

An early summer story about the historic inns along the Mississippi in Iowa was on her agenda. She would start her story in La Crosse and travel down to the Quad Cities. Her second night was at a quaint bed and breakfast just off the river in Dubuque. She had just finished taking photos along the riverwalk and was putting her equipment in her trunk when a noise caused her to turn. As she did, a person dressed in all black wearing a mask swung and hit her on the side of her head. She had no time to scream or defend herself.

Her first conscious sensation was being dropped on the ground. She was tied hand and foot, blindfolded and gagged. She felt her hands being tied to a small tree. Then, her legs were tied as well. She struggled, but was not able to move. There was only the sound of the outdoors, no sound from her abductor. Then some sort of blanket was thrown over her, and the abductor walked away.

April awoke to a voice, "Not the uppity person you were when I saw you last, huh?" The voice was familiar, though she couldn't place it. "You scream, you die." The tape was ripped from her mouth. "Who are you, and why are you doing this?" she cried. In her panic she struggled to get loose. Her reward was a slap across the face. "You scream or struggle, you die!" She felt the blindfold being untied.

The call to the Dubuque Police Department from the River's Edge Bed and Breakfast came in about noon. A young woman had checked into the B & B, but had not checked out, and all of her belongings were left behind. The police dispatcher took the name and make and model of car, and asked for a return call if the young woman showed up. The car information was put on a "not urgent" watch.

The Kansas City Police Department's call to the sheriff's department informed them of a Minnesota car licensed to a Dan Rutledge was found abandoned in a motel lot a week earlier. Could they follow up in Minnesota as they had no evidence of foul play on their end?

Haley was having lunch at the Perkins in Little Falls when Greg Ireland walked up. "Has anything happened with the stuff I found over on the state land a couple of weeks ago? Haley replied, "It has been a little slow, so I sent in the blood sample. It turns out it was human, but probably just that poacher with a cut. Nothing else has come in about any issues over there either." "Just curious", said Greg, "I haven't been back over there since, but may get over there this weekend if the weather holds."

April looked up. She immediately recognized the guy who had stalked her a couple of years ago on a story she was doing in St. Cloud. It only heightened her fear. "What do you want from me?" she asked. "You need to be taught some manners," was the response. When the knife appeared April screamed. The tape was immediately put back over her mouth. "I warned you," came the response.

April struggled as her clothing was cut from her body. Already cold from the early summer temperature, she shivered more from fear. "Now we're going to have that date that we should have had two years ago," he smiled. "Are you ready?"

The weather remained warm through the middle of May and Greg planned to do some hiking. His friend Nick was back in town and he and Greg had a couple of beers on Friday night. "Want to do a little hiking tomorrow?" asked Greg. "Sorry, I have to clean and load the truck to be ready to head out on Sunday afternoon," replied Nick. "Enjoy yourself, and don't get lost. Maybe we can get in a hike over the Memorial Day, I'll be around for four or five days."

Greg had not been back to the Beaver Falls area since he had called the sheriff's office about the blood. He parked in the same area as last time, locked his car and headed through the trees to the open area a mile distant. There was a chance of rain, but only an occasional cloud shadowed Greg.

Curiosity led him back to the spot he had

showed to Deputy Haley. To his surprise, he noticed that the area was still matted down. He looked closer at a dark spot and saw that it looked like blood. His first thought was to call Haley again, but the result would probably be the same.

Greg noticed the small areas of ground slightly disturbed, like a small animal had dug a bit. Then he saw a faint trail leading off into the forest, like something had been dragged. After about fifty feet he lost the trail.

It was about noon and the clouds were increasing, so Greg decided to head back. He figured he had covered about three miles when he decided to circle north around a big marshy area filled with tamarack trees. They had that early summer green look, returning from their dead winter appearance. The marsh ran probably a half mile from east to west and about two miles in length from north to south. Greg had headed south after losing the trail, skirting the south end of the marsh, then heading northwest.

As he came down the east side of the low area, he noticed a trail into the swamp. The trail was nothing more than the swamp grass bent in toward a slight rise in the marsh, probably about a hundred yards to the west. He had noticed the little island in the marsh before, but assumed it was inaccessible. But the extended drought in the northern half of Minnesota had dried up a lot of marshes and small lakes.

Greg often felt like an explorer when he hiked, wondering if anyone had ever walked where he hiked. He knew Native Americans had long lived in this area of the state, first the Sioux, then the Ojibwa. But, with the changing climate, some areas were accessible that had not been for years, perhaps centuries.

Greg was about to follow the faint trail into the marsh toward the small rise in the middle when he felt the first drops of rain. The decision made for him, he hustled toward his car and shelter from the rain.

The eyes followed Greg as he started in toward the mound, then watched as he turned around. Curiosity kills more than cats, thought the person behind the eyes.

Ray Strunk had spent his entire life in Central Minnesota. He grew up here, went to high school here, and then worked his entire career here. His life was the life he wanted, but to everyone else it looked boring. Ray didn't care about school, graduating with less than honors. He started working at the local boat factory and, after only twenty years, had worked his way up to shift foreman.

His was the consummate story of the Peter Principle. He disliked the college kids who worked during the summer, he disliked those with the desire to work hard, and he hated people with smiles on their faces. He had never married, and inherited the family homestead when his mother died two years earlier. Most of the people in the Sheriff's Department knew Strunk, and some had even worked with him while in high school or college.

Strunk's idea of a good time was going to a Twins game Minneapolis. It was on one of those trips from which Strunk did not return. He was reported missing when he didn't show up for work on a Monday. Cliff Devlin took the call at the sheriff's department and dispatched a car to Ray's house. The report came back with no answer at the door and no car. Though Strunk was an obstinate character, disappearing was something he had not done before.

After a cursory investigation turned up nothing, Haley put out a watch for Strunk's car, then stopped at the boat company to talk with co-workers. After learning about the Saturday Twins game, Haley contacted the police department in Big Lake. A lot of Twins fans took the train from Big Lake to be dropped off just outside the stadium, saving driving and parking problems.

Haley received word late Monday that Strunk's car was in the lot at the train station. It was only an hour trip to the train station, leaving plenty of daylight to check out the car. The car was locked and showed no sign of anything out of the ordinary. Haley considered having the car towed, but there was no proof that Strunk wasn't just on a bender in the Twin Cities.

Back in the Sheriff's Department on Tuesday morning, Haley couldn't shake the feeling that there was more here than he was seeing. He decided to check on missing persons with the Minnesota Bureau of Criminal Apprehension. Nothing recent that looked related in any way caught his eye.

Then he thought of the call a few weeks ago about the abandoned car in Kansas City. That was about another person from the area. As nothing had turned up on this end, Haley made a call to Kansas City to see if anything had happened on their end. They still had the car, but no person---or body.

Though local law enforcement departments generally were hesitant in calling the FBI, Haley's experience at the FBI training facility had given him connections. He called Special Agent

Alicia Kolovich, whom he had met during a training course the previous year.

"Hey Haley, it's been quite a while, what's new?" "Well Ms. Kolovich, perhaps I just called to see how things are going in the big city," he said.   "I know better than that," Kolovich replied. "Actually, I'm calling to pick your brain on a matter that might affect both of us," he replied.

Haley went on to talk about the disappearance of Ray Strunk, which had caused him to look into missing persons. He brought up the case of Dan Rutledge. Kolovich told him that the Rutledge case was on their radar, but had no information about Strunk. They agreed to meet for lunch the next day when Kolovich was headed up to Fargo.

Kolovich had chosen the FBI after her graduation from the University of Minnesota. She had been with the Bureau for twelve years, with the last four in St. Paul. Her biggest case was two years earlier when she was the lead agent in the heiress kidnapping. She had solved the case and brought the girl home safely. She made her career her priority and seldom did anything socially, so meeting with Haley would be as close to a social occasion as she had done in a while.

13

They met at the Black and White Cafe, an eclectic Little Falls establishment with local charm. Haley watched as the dark haired, attractive agent entered. She was almost as tall as Haley's six feet, and clearly kept in shape. All of the regulars watched her enter and sit across from him in a booth in the back.

After a little catching up, Kolovich brought out her report. She told Haley that there were 11 missing persons cases currently active in the St. Paul Region. When, and if, the Strunk case was added, it would make an even dozen. Of the 11, seven had occurred in the last three months. Another case with local ties was a report of a missing woman in Branson.

Haley brought her up to date on the Strunk case, then asked about specifics on the Rutledge case. "It's been a dead end," Kolovich said. We searched his property and found nothing to get us headed in the right direction. Our Kansas City office had nothing beyond the abandoned car near a Denny's." "I think Rutledge was principal when one of our deputies went to high school. I need to check who that was and see if there is anything to add," Haley continued. "I will let you know on that."

They agreed to meet again on Kolovich's return trip in three days. Haley hoped to be able to share additional information at that time. There were too many dead ends in both cases.

14

Haley brought out the Strunk file to see what he might have missed. Based on the length of time since Strunk's disappearance, a search of his residence and work place was next on the list.
 Haley assigned a deputy to visit the boat factory, while he took another officer along to search the Strunk home and outbuildings. Everything looked like a place where the person left expecting to return shortly.

When nothing turned up at the boat factory, including the absence of anyone knowing of any plans by Strunk, Haley decided to investigate credit cards and bank accounts. He hoped to have information ready for the return meeting with Agent Kolovich. It occurred to him that he was looking forward to seeing her again.

As Haley walked into the main department office, he was greeted with, "Call for you on two, Chief Deputy Haley." It was Eunice Daggett again, with information she would only share with 'that nice chief deputy'. "Hello Eunice, what can I do for you today?"

"Reginald found a purse yesterday down the road from our house." Haley knew that Eunice lived alone and wondered who was visiting, as her two grown children lived some distance away. "We were out for our daily walk and he found it under a bush. I'll drop it by when I come to town later today." Haley replied, "Just give it to our dispatcher at the front desk when you come." "No, I have to give it to you. It has something in it," responded Eunice.

Haley had just finished putting the Strand file together when Eunice was shown into his office. He thanked her and asked if she would like coffee or tea. "No, I have to take Reginald in for his flea and tick protection." Ah, a dog.

Eunice gave him the purse and said, "Look inside, in the hidden pocket." At first Haley found nothing, then he felt a small object through the lining. Finally he found the small opening in the lining and pulled out a key with a tag with River's Edge B & B on it. There were a few B & Bs around the area, but Bill was not familiar with one called River's Edge.

After Eunice left Haley checked the internet for River's Edge B & B. The only one he could find was down in Iowa, and he didn't think of any connection to any reports he had. He tagged the purse and planned to have it kept in an evidence locker until, and if, anything came of it.

16

It was the Thursday before Memorial Day when Kolovich and Haley met again. As they shook hands, he thought of how good she looked in the blue jeans and sweatshirt with the U of M logo. He realized she looked good in anything she wore. "Any news on your missing persons?" she asked. He reviewed everything, including finding nothing unusual in Strunk's bank accounts or emails. "Actually, I guess I have nothing."

Kolovich detailed the list of five missing persons, six including Ray Strunk, with Central Minnesota ties. "Of those, three were reported missing in Minnesota, one in Missouri, one in Iowa, and one in Wisconsin." Haley thought of the purse and figured it for a long shot, but what the heck. "The missing person report from Iowa wouldn't have anything to do with Dubuque, would it?" He could see that the long shot hit home by the reaction on Kolovich's face. "Why would you ask that?" Haley told her about the Reginald finding the purse, instantly wishing he had more information from Eunice.

Kolovich shared the information about April Stevenson disappearing in Dubuque a few weeks earlier. Haley gave her the key, knowing it was not a piece of case evidence for him, but could be a break for Kolovich's case.   "Could there be a connection between some of these cases? And, if so, what do they have in common?" he wondered. "Maybe the key is the break we are looking for," responded Kolovich. "In the meantime, could you get more on where the purse was found? We may need to search that area."

17

As promised, Nick was around on Memorial Day weekend and called Greg to see if he was in the mood for some hiking. "Where and when," responded Greg. "Let's go up to Beaver, haven't done that in a while." They started out early on Saturday morning and had looped the big marsh and heading down the east side when Greg suggested checking out the rise in the middle of the marsh. Nick seemed hesitant, "I've tried that before and got stuck in the muck." Greg convinced him that the drought would allow them passage into the middle.

They both froze as they topped the small rise in the middle of the small marsh island. On the back side of the rise was a double row of open graves. At least what looked like graves. Holes about seven feet long and three feet wide, with the dirt piled neatly along the sides.

They stepped closer to look inside and saw that the graves were empty, and were somewhat fresh. There were no markers, and nothing else to indicate why they were here. "Too weird for me," said Greg.

It took them very little time to get back to their car, about half the normal time. Neither had said anything about the graves on the thirty minute walk out of hike. "Who do we tell?" asked Greg. "I think Haley and the sheriff will think I've gone crazy." Nick suggested calling the Department of Natural Resources, which Greg later did, though he was only able to leave a message as it was Saturday.

Two days prior, Haley and Kolovich had visited Eunice Daggett to get information on where the purse was found. A thorough search of the area by Kolovich, Haley and a couple of deputies had turned up very little of interest. The usual wrappers, bags and paper, along with two tires and a deer carcass were the only items found. A box of matches from Nashville caught the eye of one of the deputies and he commented on the fact that there must still be smokers down there.

Haley had invited Kolovich to stay for dinner, which they did at the Cabin Fever eatery just north of Little Falls. Haley was delighted to spend more time with her, even though the main topic was missing persons. Unfortunately there were dozens of questions with no answers. As Kolovich left she agreed to call the following week for an update.

19

An investigative reporter for the St. Cloud Times called the sheriff's department on the Tuesday after Memorial Day with questions about the missing persons from Central Minnesota, mentioning Dan Rutledge and Ray Strunk. Haley could not share much as there was little to share. The reporter asked about possible connections.
 Though Haley had the same thought, he did not share that with the reporter.

Jodi Karnetsky grew up in Central Minnesota and attended Minnesota State University, earning a degree in graphic design. After starting her career in St. Cloud, she had accepted a job offer in Duluth four years earlier. She occasionally made her way back home, but was firmly entrenched in the Duluth social circle. She loved the Canal Park bar scene, with trips up to Lutsen during the ski season.

It was Memorial Day, and a warm sunny day on the waterfront. Jodi had spent the day with friends barhopping in Canal Park, and found herself heading home a little later than she had originally planned. Work tomorrow would come soon enough and she wanted to get to bed early. As she drove along Superior Street, she heard a voice say, "I have a gun pointed at the back of your head. If you don't do exactly as I say, your life is over."

The voice directed her to drive north along old highway 61 toward Two Harbors, then to pull into the parking lot of a vacated restaurant overlooking the lake. "Please don't hurt me," gasped Jodi as the rag covered her face and everything went black.

21

On the Tuesday morning after Memorial Day, the Minnesota Department of Natural Resources office receptionist listened to the message left by Greg Ireland over the weekend. She filled out an incident report and put it in the inbox for the officers to investigate. With Memorial Day lake usage being quite high, the inbox had several items in it, and the report from Greg and Nick ended up on the bottom.

Haley had taken a three day weekend, his first in many years, and that meant catching up on Tuesday morning. For that reason he arrived at the department before 7 AM. As expected, a lot had happened over the weekend. A couple of burglaries, a keg party with minors, and a relatively minor traffic accident which all could be handled by other deputies.

It was time to pull everything together on the missing person's reports. After collecting all available information, Haley came to the conclusion that he really didn't have much. The main problem being that he had no evidence of a crime being committed.

After spending most of the day reading and re-reading all of the reports, Haley called Kolovich. He expressed his frustration with the lack of credible information in each of the cases. "I can only add to the confusion," shared Kolovich. "The key found by Ms. Daggett was a match to the B & B in Dubuque." "Now we have three cases with a connection to the area, but nothing to prove that we even have cases," muttered Haley. That, in a nutshell, was where they found themselves.

23

Kolovich invited Haley to meet in the St. Paul office of the FBI the next afternoon to compare notes. By noon Haley had made the seventy-five mile trip and stopped for a light lunch before heading over to meet Kolovich. She had a room set up with boards of info on each of the missing person cases, including Ray Strunk and Dan Rutledge.

"We've had agents investigating in each of the cases as because of the probable interstate connections. One thing that seems tie these cases together is North Central Minnesota," Kolovich said as she pointed to each case. "Rutledge disappeared in Kansas, but was from your area. Emily Vandenburg disappeared in Missouri, but grew up here. And April's key showed up in your back yard." And Haley knew that the Strunk case certainly evolved in his jurisdiction.

As Haley and Kolovich stood and looked at the scant evidence, the same thought formed for each of them: there was a connection, but knowing that didn't seem to help at all. "Besides having no bodies, there has to be something else here that we are missing," muttered Haley. "And if there is a connection between these cases, what is the motive?"

Haley was happy to have Kolovich suggest that they adjourn for the day and catch dinner at Mickey's Diner in St. Paul. The Diner was a place Haley liked to stop at each time he found himself working in St. Paul. His dad had taken him there for a malt when he was a boy, and he was hooked. He was able to get Kolovich talk a little more about her life, and less about the cases this time. One thing he discovered is that they both loved spending time outdoors.

24

Haley met Kolovich at 8 AM at FBI headquarters the next day after spending the night with his sister in White Bear Lake. Before getting settled, Kolovich informed Haley of another disappearance with ties to the area. A young woman, Jodi Karnetsky, disappeared in Duluth over the weekend. Though she lived in Duluth, she had attended Minnesota State and worked in the area before moving. Local police had found her car abandoned north of Duluth, but no clues indicated where she had gone.

Kolovich had been assigned full time to these missing person cases, and it looked like another had to be added. "We don't need more cases, we need some indication of a direction to go. Can you get some time off your other duties to join us on this as it obviously involves your department?"   Haley made a call to Sheriff Rafferty, and was able to clear his schedule after going back to wrap up some loose ends that afternoon. He told Kolovich that he would be back at FBI headquarters the next morning.

    In the morning, Haley stopped at the
sheriff's department to check his
messages before heading to FBI
headquarters. Along with a request for
information on a missing person from the
Duluth PD, the rest was the usual routine
of calls and emails. Cliff Devlin joked
about Haley spending time with "the
Feeb gal" and asked if they were making
any headway. Haley gave him an
update. It was good to see Devlin start
to take more of an interest in his job. He
seemed to be more interested in his
antique collections than on police work
most of the time.

Haley quickly assigned follow up by other
deputies and headed to St. Paul. As he
walked out, a call came into dispatch
from the DNR.   Devlin took the message
and dropped it in Haley's inbox.

26

"Let's take this back to square one," suggested Kolovich once Haley and the rest of the investigative team congregated in the evidence room. "Let's assume that there is a connection between each of these disappearances and try to pinpoint a direction." The team spent the next hour setting scenarios in which the cases could be tied. The only obvious conclusion was that, if connected, someone from the area, or formerly from the area, was involved. With that said, there was nothing else.

Kolovich suggested doing a detailed background of each of the missing persons with the hope that some connection would pop up. Haley picked up the file on the Strunk missing person case and took it with him for the weekend. Kolovich set a Monday morning meeting with the direction of

having all background information
available at the time.

27

Haley got back to his office in time to look over his notes on the Strunk case, and to clear his desk for the weekend. He saw the information from the DNR and thought back to his visit to Beaver Falls with Greg Ireland. According to the DNR, someone had done some digging on a high point in the big marsh. Because of the recent rains, they had not been able to get into the marsh. However, they did have a photo taken in a flyover. The message also indicated that the DNR was going to send an officer in on the following Monday if there was no more rain.

The photo showed elongated holes dug with the dirt alongside. Because of foliage it was difficult to see much else. Haley called the DNR office and asked for a report once they had an onsite visual of the digging.

The DNR message also included the person reporting the digging, one Greg Ireland. Haley decided to call Greg to see if he could shed more light on the report. His call led to Greg's voicemail and he asked for a call back.

Haley received a call back from Greg on Saturday morning. "Sorry I didn't get back to you last night, but I had to work until midnight." Haley asked Greg about his report to the DNR and made some notes. He was looking forward to the DNR report on Monday.

28

Haley spent Sunday making a timeline of the life of Ray Strunk. He took a little break in the afternoon to watch the Twins as early June was too early to start thinking about the Vikings. The Twins were only six games behind Detroit and hope was still springing eternal.

Ray Strunk had lived a very uneventful life. He was an average student, at best, in high school and was an uninvolved adult. Haley called a couple of retired teachers and found that although Strunk was not a good student, he was not a discipline problem. It was more of a lack of inertia problem.

Calls to contacts at the boat factory amounted to more of the same. Strunk managed to move up only because everyone else had retired or moved on, and no one wanted the job as late shift foreman. The only item of note was that Strunk had some problems with some of the summer help, trying to fire them, only to be overruled by management.

29

Monday morning saw the investigation restarting in St. Paul with updates from all task force members. After background data was shared on each of the missing persons cases, loose connections could be made between the cases involving Emily Vandenburg, Dan Rutledge, April Stevenson, Ray Strunk, and Jodi Karnetsky. Each of the missing persons had a tie to Stearns County, specifically the St. Cloud area. However, what that tie was, remained to be discovered.

"If we're assuming that these cases are related, and if we assume a crime has been committed, we have to find a common denominator," Kolovich stated. "Maybe a former student of Rutledge who ended up in St. Cloud," shared Albin Murphy, one of the investigators. "Or Rutledge spent some time in St. Cloud and had a run in with someone," said

Haley. "Unfortunately, that's the circle we find ourselves in right now," said Kolovich in disgust. "We're still looking at a brick wall until we get something concrete."

Haley's phone chirped to the tune of the Beach Boys and he noted the call was from the DNR. "Gotta take this," he said, stepping out into the hall. After five minutes he was back and told the rest of the group about the call. "According to the DNR, someone dug several holes that looked like graves, but they were all empty. The investigating DNR officer saw no other evidence of human presence, not even a shovel."
  Haley added the he would share the report with photos when he received a copy from the DNR.

As they broke for lunch, Haley told Kolovich about Greg Ireland's report from almost a month earlier about the matted area and the blood. He also brought up the truck that Eunice Daggett claimed to have seen. "I didn't really want a bunch of dead people in graves, but thought it might be the lead we were looking for."

30

He wondered about the lack of news coverage of the missing persons. It seemed that newspaper people were no longer interested in tips. He had given the reporter for the St. Cloud Times a hint that the missing persons should be checked out, but nothing had appeared in the paper. He had seen Chief Deputy Haley out looking at his playground, but nothing had happened there either.

Perhaps he had to provide another clue.

31

When Haley got back from St. Paul he had a message to call Eunice Daggett. "Hi Eunice, Deputy Haley here," he announced. "Deputy Haley, the strangest thing happened. I found a ring in the mail today." She proceeded to tell Haley about going out to get her mail and finding a Minnesota State class ring in her mail box.

Haley went out to visit Eunice to pick up the ring. He also wanted to see if she remembered more about the truck she had seen a couple of times, and if she had seen it lately. She hadn't, and just remembered it was white and was what she called a small semi and trailer.

Back at his office, Haley checked out the ring. It couldn't be a coincidence that the initials inside were JLK, the exact initials of their missing person from Duluth, Jodi Lynn Karnetsky. Though

Eunice had handled the ring, Haley hoped to find other prints and sent it through for processing and then called Kolovich. "Could you make a trip up here tomorrow? I have something to show you."

32

By the time Kolovich arrived the next day, Haley had discovered that the ring indeed belonged to Jodi Karnetsky, and that there were no fingerprints other than those of Eunice Daggett. After a search of the ditches along the road from the Daggett house, past the area where Eunice had seen the truck, they found exactly nothing. As they arrived at their cars, the rain started to fall.

"We're fortunate that there has not been any public concern over these cases," said Haley as they had lunch in at The Fort in Fort Ripley. "But we may have to alert the public in order to generate some tips," commented Kolovich. "This is the most confusing collection of cases our office has handled in quite some time."

Upon return to Haley's office they looked over the DNR report sent over. It was pretty much what Haley had reported, along with photos from the flyover and from the officer on the ground. "Chief Deputy, look at these photos side by side. Are they taken from the same side, and if so, doesn't there appear to be a change from one to the next?" It did indeed look like an additional hole had been added between the flyover and the onsite photo. A meeting with the DNR officer was the next step. Unfortunately, he would not be back until the next afternoon.

"With this rain it will become impossible to cross that bog for another few days, but we need to get a close up look at those holes." Haley said as they tried to determine their next course of action. "We need something positive to happen to get us moving in the right direction."

Kolovich decided to stay in Little Falls at the Waller B & B so they could get back at the investigation the next day. She had previously stayed there and loved the authentic remodeling that had been done to the old house.

After each of them took care of some routine matters, they met at Haley's office at ten the next day to review and get ready for the meeting with the DNR officer. "I almost want to find a body, at least we'd have somewhere to start, though we haven't had much experience with murder investigations up in this neck of the woods." Kolovich responded, "Be careful what you wish for."

33

J. D. Dalrymple had worked with the Minnesota DNR for over 25 years, mostly in the southern part of the state. He had recently transferred to the area to be closer to family. He told Kolovich and Haley that he was not too familiar with the area, but that he spent several hours in Beaver Falls the past week. "It was the darnedest thing, a bunch of holes dug in that little rise in the swamp. It looked like a cemetery waiting for bodies."

Dalrymple distributed the photos he had taken and went over what he had seen on site. "Real weird, nothing in the holes, and nothing else in the area. I saw a few footprints, but the rain made it impossible to determine anything about them. I even poked a stick into a couple of the holes and didn't hit anything in that sandy soil."

Kolovich and Haley decided that there was nothing else to get from Dalrymple. "I can't see what this might have to do with our cases. Do you believe in UFOs?" asked Haley. She chuckled, "That's about as much sense as I can make out of this whole thing. But something just isn't right, and I can't figure out what it is."

"Let's review. We have a 'sort of' cemetery with holes that look like graves. We have case files on Dan Rutledge, Ray Strunk, April Stevenson, Emily Vandenburg, and now Jodi Karnetsky," Kolovich said as they returned to Haley's office. "If nothing turns up by tomorrow, I think we should check out those excavations ourselves."

The timing of the discovery of the "graves" while active investigations were happening with missing persons was perhaps nothing more than a coincidence. "Do you believe in coincidences?" Kolovich responded, "I've always been told that there is no such thing in police work."

34

Lyle "Butthead" Koslo had gone to school locally and was a jack of all trades and a master of one. Unfortunately, the one was drinking. He had worked at a variety of jobs, ran for office a couple of times, and there were rumors about petty theft. Customers at the local drinking establishments knew that you could talk Lyle into doing just about anything for a few drinks.

It was one of those nights when Lyle agreed to steal some turkeys and turn them loose in city hall. He heard the laughter as he left the bar, though he thought the laughter was because this was a good joke. He could hear the laughter until he started his old beater and headed out of town to the turkey farm.

35

"Special Agent Kolovich, we have another missing person." Haley then told her about a deputy finding Lyle "Butthead" Koslo's car in the middle of Highway 28 out past Swanville. It was another case of a person gone missing, but showing no evidence of foul play. "Lyle has done some strange things, but he's usually around somewhere."

"I'm getting to feel like a broken record here, but there has to be some connection," said Kolovich as she slumped in the chair across from Haley's desk. "Let's dig into Koslo's background to see if we can find a tie to any of the others. And, could you see if the DNR could have Dalrymple check for any changes in those graves?" Haley sent one of his deputies over to the DNR office to see if Dalrymple could show him the site and check for changes. They both knew that a change out at Beaver

Falls would tie the proverbial knot as far as connections go.

They spent the next few hours going through Koslo's background, looking for anything that would tie him to the other cases. Haley was just about to pull the files when his phone buzzed. He took the call, listened, and hung up. "Well, forget Koslo being a case tied to the others. A turkey farmer out past Swanville found him sleeping out behind one of the barns this morning.
 Apparently some of the local barley pop crowd talked him into stealing some turkeys, and his alcohol consumption caught up with him before he could do the deed."

After lunch Kolovich and Haley met and compared the photos taken earlier with those taken by the deputy today. "No changes, and my deputy said that it appeared that nothing had been disturbed since the last rain," said Haley.
 "He didn't do any other investigation, as he wasn't sure we wanted him to do

other than take pictures." Kolovich suggested going out the next day with the evidence kit to look at the site closer, perhaps do some digging.

Greg and Nick were having a beer and planning a canoe trip in the Boundary Waters Canoe Area, one of the best wilderness spots in the world, according to National Geographic. It was only about a four hour trip to get there, in northern Minnesota just up past Duluth. "It would be a good time to get my truck detailed," said Greg. "I have had it for almost a year and need to get my name on it. I also need to get it cleaned again." "You clean that truck more often than I clean my car, and since you said you aren't smoking any more, it should not need it as often," said Greg.

They talked a little about the "graveyard" that they had discovered out at Beaver Falls. Greg told Nick about the call from Haley. "Pretty weird stuff," said Nick.
 "The nut cases are coming closer to home it seems!"

The call came in at 8:30 the next morning. A body had been found in some state land about ten miles north of Eunice Daggett's house, and about five miles from Beaver Falls. The body of the young woman, buried in a shallow grave, was found by a hiker and his dog.
 Because of their investigations into the series of disappearances, calls went out to Kolovich and Haley.

The body, tentatively identified as Jodi Karnetsky, was nude. It appeared that she had been strangled by a belt, possible her own. There did not appear to be any injuries, except on her wrists and ankles, where she had been restrained. There was also an indication of sexual assault. One unusual aspect was two parallel lines across her forehead, each about two inches long.
 They appeared to have been made with a marker.

"Now we have a body, which means that the innocence of the disappearances has changed," said Haley as he and Kolovich watched the medical examiner finish her investigation at the site. "Unfortunately, if they're connected, we're going to find more bodies."

38

To add to the game he was playing, he decided to throw off law enforcement by "hiding" Jodi's body where it could be found outside of Beaver Falls. They were getting too close to his little "graveyard". He had a few more names on his list, so he needed the investigation rerouted for a little longer. The investigation of the Karnetsky case would give him the time to move on with his plans. Just another couple of weeks and he would disappear like smoke in the wind.

39

As Kolovich and Haley arrived back at the sheriff's office, Cliff Devlin told them that the DNR had done another flyover and had some photos. He reported that he had filed them for their information later as the new case had come up.   "I heard it was the Karnetsky girl," said Devlin, "that sure sucks! You expect that down in the Cities, but not here."

"The Duluth Bureau Office is sending us all the information on Jodi's disappearance from their end," said Kolovich. "It includes interviews with her roommates, friends who she had been out with, a former boyfriend, and her neighbors."

After going through all the interviews, looking at possible timelines, and reviewing the investigation into Jodi's car, they had nothing that remotely looked like a strong clue. Jodi was not a smoker, but there was a slight cigarette odor in her car. It was clear that who had taken her had been very careful. "I think we should look for a connection on this end," said Haley. "If it is connected to these other disappearances, then there has to be something in her past from her that will give us a direction." Kolovich agreed, "I've been thinking the same thing, being taken in Duluth and brought back here just makes that more than a coincidence."

40

The FBI connection was able to get the autopsy on Jodi Karnetsky moved to the front of the order. It was scheduled for the next morning in St. Paul.
 Kolovich and Haley planned to be in attendance to get firsthand information about the last hours of their victim.

"I'm planning to head down to the Twin Cities tonight." said Haley, "Want to catch a late dinner at Manny's?" That sounded good to Kolovich. Haley was becoming more than just a fellow officer.
 "Let's plan on it, maybe about 7:30?"
 They agreed and Haley headed for the office while Kolovich headed back to the Cities, hoping to beat the rush hour traffic.

As usual, Manny's was busy and the fare was excellent. Kolovich and Haley talked about the case for a while, then discussed a little about their respective pasts. They shared an enjoyment of the outdoors, especially hiking as a form of stress relief. Haley suggested a little hiking together "after we close this case." Kolovich agreed without hesitation.

41

The Karnetsky autopsy revealed very little. The victim had been killed by strangulation shortly after her abduction, probably in 24 to 48 hours. She had been deceased prior to her burial. There was evidence of a sexual assault, although the perpetrator wore a condom.

In recounting the evidence in the case, they found several aspects to be followed up on, but no strong leads. Though the victim had been restrained, the method of the restraint was no longer on the body. It appeared a rope had been used, but unless the small fibers on her wrist were identifiable, that was a dead end as well. The marks on the forehead could have been made by any over the counter marker. "Let's do some background on Jodi in the Central Minnesota area," suggested Kolovich.

"I'll run a law enforcement check while

you check out her time after high school in St. Cloud." They were meeting at the FBI office and agreed to get back together in an hour to compare notes.

"No contact with law enforcement at any time in her past according to the background check other than a teenage party where alcohol was present while Jodi was in high school," said Kolovich. "Anything show up on your investigation?"   Haley's information included high school and college activities, with no red flags. "I am waiting for a call back from security at Minnesota State, but if there is nothing in the law enforcement database, I don't expect much there either."

"We need to try to locate some of her friends or roommates from college to see if that gives us something.   I'm going to call a friend in the registrar's office to see if I can find housing information for Jodi." As Haley left to follow that trail, Kolovich tried to cross reference Jodi with the other missing persons.   Maybe

there was something they had missed,
some connection there to be found.

42

Lunch at Mickey's Diner was followed by another session back at the FBI office. "I have some names of roommates in the Karnetsky case. Let's see if we can track any of them down. There are six names, though we don't know if any have changed names which would make them harder to find." Haley handed Kolovich three of the names and they started the process of trying to contact the roommates.

They were able to find two of the roommates at home and found out that Jodi had a stalker while at Minnesota State. She never reported it to the police because a couple of guy friends had a talk with the guy and that seemed to end it. The roommates knew very little about the guy, having never seen him. They were not even sure who the guy friends of Jodi were. They were sure that the stalker was not a student at the school.

"If we just had missing females we could follow the stalker angle," said Haley. "That is, if there is a connection to the cases." They were on the same page in that thinking, believing that the cases were related. "We both believe they are, but what is the connection?" wondered Kolovich.

43

Haley received a call back from security at Minnesota State stating that they have periodic calls about stalkers, and had three reports while Jodi Karnetsky was enrolled. None of the reports had been filed by Jodi. Haley asked for names of the other three young women who had filed reports, and a copy of the report. It would be emailed over in the next hour.

Kolovich wondered aloud about the graves found by hikers out at Beaver Lake. "I sent a deputy out to look at the digging site. Since we couldn't get there earlier because of the rain, and then the Karnetsky case, I wanted more info", said Haley. "I asked him to call from the site if he could get reception. If he was able to get across the swamp, he should be there soon."

As Haley was about to head back to his

office, the Beach Boys sound was heard. "Haley here, what do you have? How far down? And the pile? Thanks." "My deputy says that the holes are empty and he dug down about a foot. He also moved most of two of the piles of dirt next to the holes and found nothing." Kolovich responded, "I get the feeling that someone is playing with our heads and is doing a good job of it!"

Haley headed back up to his office with the agreement to meet again the next day, with the location depending on what showed up reports from the college security office. Kolovich also planned to rework each of the cases through the FBI database to see in anything new came up.

44

At Kolovich's suggestion, they met at Haley's office the next day. Both had information to share that would possible shed light on their cases. An FBI scan had showed that the earring found at the beginning of this series of missing persons was a tentative match to the jewelry in the apartment of Emily Vandenberg. "We also found out that April Stevenson spent some time doing a story in St. Cloud a couple of years ago," Kolovich added.

"We need to look at those stalker reports from Minnesota State. Have you received the reports from the security office?" "I need to call them. Apparently getting them in an hour was just a way to put me off. I'll call them again and mention your office this time."

They received the reports from the college security office 15 minutes later.

The reports were complete, with one exception. The names of the women filing the reports had been blacked out citing privacy issues. It looked like another call would be needed. In each case the stalker had been described as approximately 30 years old, white, about 5 feet, 10 inches tall and a medium build. The stalker had never threatened the women, and had never done anything physical. He would ask for a date, then not accept "no" for an answer. He had never been identified.

It seemed to be a dead end, because once law enforcement was called, the stalker disappeared each time. "Just to be sure we cover all the bases," said Haley, "Let's get the names of the women." A phone call led to an official request to the office of the college legal representative. The information would be available the next day.

45

The bombshell landed the next day when Haley received the names of the women who had reported stalkers at Minnesota State. When he shared the names with Kolovich, she responded, "We have our break!" One of the names was Willis "Billy" Danvers. Willis Danvers was the name of the person reported missing in Wisconsin a little over a month ago.

"We need to get in touch with the other two names on the list from the security guys at Minnesota State as soon as possible." Kolovich called her office and directed someone to find the addresses of the women immediately.

A call to the Ellsworth Police Department in Wisconsin led to a conversation with Davis Beckwith, Chief Detective. "We are at our wits end on that case.   One day Willis is at work, the next day no one can find her. We found her car just outside of town behind the old Holiday Station.   Absolutely nothing, no clues to be found. She had just started a job with the new clinic in town, doing something with computers. We have not found her phone, and there was nothing in the phone records anyway."

"We have the FBI involved with several missing person cases here in Minnesota, and this one may be related." Haley continued by asking if Beckwith could follow up with the family to see if they knew of any harassment or threats to Willis after she returned from Minnesota State. Beckwith would get back to them by the next day with any information from the family.

By the time they finished their conversation with Detective Beckwith, Kolovich had the information on the other two women. One, Susan Stensrud, was serving in the Air Force, currently stationed in Alaska. The other, Carmen Delaquez, lived and worked in the Twin

Cities. A call to her listed phone went unanswered.

46

Kolovich and Haley arrived at the Delaquez apartment at 6:45 that evening. There was no one home, and still no answer on her phone. A call to her place of employment indicated that Carmen had left at 5:30. And no, the staff member did not know if Carmen had plans after work. Kolovich put out an APB on Carmen's car, to notify her if it was spotted. Meanwhile, she and Haley waited at the apartment building.

At 7:30 Carmen Delaquez arrived home and was greeted by Special Agent Kolovich and Chief Deputy Haley. Once she got past the worry of an issue with a family member, Carmen asked what she could do for the two of them. "We need to talk to you about the stalker you reported a few years back at Minnesota State," replied Alicia. "I have not seen or heard from that creep since I reported him to the college security officers. That was five years ago."

Kolovich and Haley decided to err on the side of caution and told Delaquez about the missing persons, including that two others who had reported stalkers had disappeared. "We would like to have an agent monitor your movements for the near future at least," said Kolovich.
 "Keep your doors locked and be sure who is outside your door before you open it. You can reach me at this number 24-7. We are sorry to put you in this situation, but until we can solve these missing person cases, we want you to be safe."

After waiting until the agent assigned to Carmen arrived, Kolovich and Haley decided to catch a late dinner and plan their next moves. "I will alert the Air Force in regard to Ms. Stensrud, and let them decide the proper course of action."
 Haley added, "Have them let us know if she will be coming home on leave any time soon."

47

The following morning Haley arrived back in his office to catch up on messages and, upon entering, met the new summer intern, Margot Cosgrove. She was a petite, dark haired 20 year old who appeared to spend a lot of time working out. Margot would be starting her senior year in college in pursuit of a career in law enforcement, with an eye on a career in the FBI. Haley hoped that the fact that Cosgrove's uncle was a county commissioner had not greased the wheels for this internship, but his first impression was that she was willing to work and wanted to learn everything.

Haley remembered that he was the person directed to give Ms. Cosgrove her schedule of duties. He set up a schedule for the next week with her spending a day in each area of the office, starting with dispatch and Cliff Devlin. He gave her a couple of cases to organize during down time.

48

Letting law enforcement find the body of Jodi Karnetsky was a smooth move on his part, he decided. Though they were following the college stalker path, he felt they were no closer to catching him.
 That was good, because he wasn't done.
 He had more moments to "share" with a few others. And he wasn't planning to get caught.

He couldn't afford to get careless knowing that Haley had called in the FBI, but he was enjoying his short time with each person on his list. It was amazing how each of them seemed to feel remorse once they realized he was in full control.

49

In a late morning phone conversation, Kolovich and Haley shared the latest information. Detective Beckwith had reported that Willis Danvers had not mentioned any calls, notes, or letters of harassment to family members. Though Kolovich had not received word back from the Air Force, they felt it unlikely that any attempts had been made in that arena. But they would follow up if they did not hear in the next couple of days.

It was midafternoon when Margot Cosgrove knocked on Haley's door. She told him about a strange call into dispatch and asked him to listen to the tape. "You need to look for bodies in the river." The voice was muffled and a trace on the number showed that it came from a burner phone. "Okay, my first day and I get a call like this. Is this a regular thing in law enforcement?" asked

Cosgrove. "No, it's not a usual thing. The problem is that we don't know if it is a crank call, or if it's related to the missing person cases we have on our desks."

The river in the call might be referring to the Mississippi River, which flowed only a half mile from Haley's office. But with the Mississippi flowing through, or along, several states, a message to look in the river was like saying, "Look for a needle in a haystack." Haley put little credibility in the call, but dispatched the water patrol to do a river run twenty miles up, and down, the river.

Haley called Kolovich about the message after dispatching the water patrol. She said she would run an air search on the river as well. It might be nothing, but that's really what they had anyway on these cases. "Let's meet tomorrow morning in your office," said Alicia. "I need to be in Brainerd for a meeting in the afternoon."

50

As soon as Kolovich arrived in Haley's office the next morning, he showed her pictures of the 'find' in the river. The water patrol had found a mannequin dressed to look like a man floating in the river about 15 miles south of Little Falls. The mannequin was unmarked, there were no labels in the clothing, and no note to say it was a practical joke, or any evidence it was put there by the person who called dispatch the day before.

"We need to get a look into the closets of Dan Rutledge and Ray Strunk. Both guys were single so it will be hard to get anyone to identify the clothing as theirs if that is the case." Kolovich had another thought, "Any identification on the mannequin?" "No, and the problem is that the Munsingwear factory closed years ago in Little Falls, so many homes in the area have mannequins on display."

"Let's meet in the morning on my way back from Brainerd. You'll probably have information on the clothing sizes from both missing men by then. We can figure out our next move after having that information." They grabbed lunch at the Black and White Café in Little Falls, then headed their separate ways.

51

The clothing matched the size and styles found in Dan Rutledge's closet. The problem was that Dan Rutledge went missing in Kansas City. If the mannequin's clothes were truly a clue, and if the clothes belonged to Dan Rutledge, this just got a whole lot crazier, thought Haley. He couldn't wait to get Kolovich's take on the matter.

It was Margot Cosgrove's day to shadow Haley, so she sat in on the meeting with Kolovich. After Haley shared the information about Rutledge's clothing basically matching the clothes on the mannequin, Kolovich indicated that if the clothes did indeed belong to Rutledge, the cases all had to be related. "I think that we need to find out how all of these missing person cases are connected. We need to get everything we can on each missing person and create a map calendar. Perhaps it will show what all of the victims have in common. Or what locations they have in common."

Cosgrove asked if she could pose a question. Certainly, she was told. "I was reading through the cases and it seems like they are connected. The reason I think so is because of the clues that you have found seem to lead back to this area. I think the mannequin is a real clue. I saw notes about the key and the jewelry, so the Karnetsky case also ended back here."

"You may have a career in law enforcement with thinking like that," said Haley. "I think that Special Agent Kolovich and I have come to that same conclusion." "So, is the guy trying to get caught? He made that call, and probably dropped the purse and put the ring in the mailbox to be found, too." That was the big question, or was it a smokescreen to get Kolovich and Haley moving in the wrong direction?

"Let's get that timeline set up on each of

the missing victims, then cross reference to see where and when they might have crossed paths. That might give us a location where each of the victims met our perp."   They both wondered if they were right in guessing that there was only one perpetrator.

52

Haley started, "Here's what we have so far. We have victims with ties to the area, either prior to, or after, their abduction.   So, I believe we have to go with the premise that our perp is from this area. However, several of the abductions took place a significant distance away. That would indicate the flexibility to travel." Kolovich interjected, "Or could indicate a second perpetrator."

"Although we have indicators that show a connection with this area, we still only have one body. If we agree that the victims were murdered, and have an area connection, where are the bodies?" Haley continued, "I keep coming back to the empty graves out at Beaver Falls. Is there a message there as well?"

Margot Cosgrove, who was sitting in on the discussion, asked, "Who digs graves and leaves them empty? Maybe the kidnapper planned to bury the bodies there, but decided not to when he discovered that the site had been found."

Haley wondered aloud, "Each time we have planned a visit to the 'graveyard' something comes up. It rains, or we get a clue, or a body shows up. Maybe we need to finally look at it ourselves and decide whether to cross it off the list."

Haley contacted the DNR to request an officer and an all-terrain vehicle for the next morning. He and Kolovich would check out the site in the marsh to see for themselves what was there. Kolovich invited Haley and Cosgrove to come along for a bite to eat. They ended up at Eagle's Landing Golf Course, about half way between Brainerd and Little Falls. It was a chance to sit outside, relax, and plan their next moves.

53

Haley's phone rang at 11:30 that evening. It was Kolovich. "There was an attempted break in at the apartment of Carmen Delaquez. She called the agent watching outside her apartment and 911. Our agent was upstairs in about 90 seconds and found a pry bar on the balcony, but nothing else."   Further investigation showed a ladder lying along the next building which could have been used to reach the second floor balcony. It was with some other equipment a painting crew had left at the end of the day.

Haley asked Kolovich whether they should go down to be part of the investigation, or to continue with plans to investigate the graves. "Something you said yesterday, or earlier today, about diversions always happening when we were considering going out to the graveyard. This seems to be one of those diversions, so let's continue with our plans.   I will see you in the morning at 8 at the DNR Office."

54

Officer Dalrymple was ready to go when Kolovich and Haley arrived at the DNR Office a little before 8 the next morning. The drive out to Beaver Falls and to the edge of the marsh took about 45 minutes. The hike through the marsh to the rise took about 15 minutes.
 Dalrymple was the first to crest the rise and he stopped in his tracks as he looked at the graves. As Haley stepped around, he noted that one of the graves had been filled. The rest were, like before, empty with neat piles along each one.

As Agent Kolovich stepped up to look, her first thought was not to touch anything. "Before we do anything, let's think about what level of forensic evaluation we want here." Haley agreed, but suggested that a closer look should be taken before dragging out a large group of people for what may be nothing.

Keeping their distance to outside of ten feet from the covered grave, they looked for anything in the area that would give them any insight. At the base of the grave, Haley noticed a small white object sticking out of the dirt. A closer look showed parts of words written in red ink.

Agent Kolovich made the decision to pull out the paper. "Probably not going to find what you are looking for down below," was printed boldly on the paper. After putting the paper in an evidence bag, Kolovich asked Haley what he thought. "It looks like someone knew we were going to look at this area. I suggest we get some shovels and see if anything is under this dirt. I'll call for a couple of deputies to help search the area."

About a foot down they discovered a sack with a newspaper inside. The paper was opened to the story from the St. Cloud Times about the missing persons.

"Okay, this is getting crazier all the time. Either the person, or persons, responsible for the disappearances is playing with us, or someone who knew we were coming out here is playing a sick joke." "I have to believe it's the person involved in the missing persons' cases," concluded Haley. "The newspaper article and the note were both aimed at us."

Going down another foot in the grave turned up nothing. The question was, was the person who planted the note and the newspaper daring Kolovich and Haley to catch him, or was it an effort to point them in the wrong direction? Leaving the deputies to complete a thorough search of the area, they headed back to the sheriff's department.

55

After a quick lunch, Kolovich and Haley met with the deputies to review everything they had up to this point.
 "We made the assumption that these cases are related and that they tie to this area. I think that we need a few more bodies helping track down every detail of our missing persons. I'm going to get a couple of agents running computer checks on everything from class rings to where they bought their cars."

Before they broke for the day, Kolovich told Haley that there was no further evidence on the attempted break-in at the Delaquez apartment. The protection detail would stay in place, though inside the apartment building itself. The door to the balcony had been secured from the inside.

A burger and a beer at Johnny C's in Little Falls following a long day somewhat tempered their frustration. Both Kolovich and Haley would have liked to down another few beers, but wanted to be ready to go the next morning when the extra agents would be sharing anything that they found.

56

At 7:30 the next morning, Haley had coffee ready when Kolovich showed up. They had everything set up when Cliff Devlin stuck his head in to let them know that the agents from the Twin Cities had arrived. Kolovich introduced Agents Norgaard and Fitzpatrick. Arn Norgaard was a veteran of 22 years currently on light duty because of an injury suffered in an arrest a month earlier. Liz Fitzpatrick was in her second year with the FBI, and had developed a reputation of someone with drive and determination.

After summarizing the case to bring everyone up to date, including the two deputies assigned to the case, Kolovich asked Norgaard and Fitzpatrick to share what they had discovered. Norgaard started by reporting on credit card use. "There are no common shopping locations, vacation areas, large purchases, or anything of that sort. We have only a couple of instances where two of the victims could have been in the same place at the same time."

Fitzpatrick followed with information about phone records and indicated, "There are no recorded calls between any of the missing persons. However, several of them received calls from burner cell phones in the months prior to their disappearance. Each of those calls were less than a minute in length. Further checking indicated that the burner phones were all purchased in the St. Cloud area. I haven't been able to get the dates and locations of the purchases, but hope to get more on that today."

"Agent Fitzpatrick, did the calls from the burner phones include calls to April Stevenson and Emily Vandenburg?" asked Haley. A quick look concluded that yes, they too had received calls. That tied the missing persons' cases in Missouri and Iowa to the cases in the area. Only two of the missing persons did not receive calls from the burner phones, Ray Strunk and Jodi Karnetsky. "I am not sure what that means, but both are definitely tied to this area," said Haley. Perhaps a pay phone was used in the other two cases he thought.

57

The deputies assigned to the search reported finding nothing within a fifty foot circle around the graves, nor did they find anything along the route into the graveyard. Haley paged Cliff Devlin and asked him to bring in all the photos from the marsh area taken from the air over the past year. "We need to see if there is anything of interest in a wider area of the marsh."

"What kind of message is there in seven empty graves? We have five victims of assumed abduction, six if you count Jodi Karnetsky. Was there a grave ready for each of them? And why dig a grave if you plan to put the body elsewhere?" Kolovich looked at the team for answers, of which none were available.

Margot Cosgrove brought the DNR photos into the conference room. She looked around at the stacks of files and the diagrams on the sheets tacked to the walls. "Anything else you need in here?" "Maybe you could give us a few clues, we're a little short along that line right now." Haley said it, but everyone else agreed. The frustration again set in.

Margot asked Haley and Kolovich about Greg Ireland. "I noticed that early on in these cases, his name came up a few times. He and his friend Nick made reports a couple of times. I was talking to Cliff in Dispatch about it and he said I should mention my curiosity to you guys."

Haley said the thought had occurred to him as well, but that he felt that he knew Greg Ireland well enough to not consider him a suspect. He also didn't think that Greg and his buddy were the type to mess with an investigation by putting the letter in the grave. Kolovich decided to have both Ireland and Dekich checked for any flags, not disagreeing with Haley but deciding to be sure nothing was overlooked.

Margot asked to speak to Haley in private and asked, "Do you have any policy about departmental dating?"

Haley said that there was none, and wondered why. "Devlin asked me out and I am not sure I want to date him, but thought I would check just in case."

"Maybe wait until your internship is over, then you can decide and not worry about any comfort issues on the job no matter which way you choose to go."

58

Mavis Bullard had retired from a career in law enforcement, including a stint as police chief in St. Mark. St. Mark was a small town in Western Stearns County, one of the more than one dozen towns in Stearns County with the "first name" of Saint. The names were courtesy of the German heritage in Central Minnesota, specifically German Catholic.

Bullard had served as police chief in St. Mark for 19 years before retiring five years earlier and settling in St. Cloud. She had her routine of volunteering at the St. Cloud Hospital every Tuesday and Thursday, and on Wednesdays at the local food bank. Though never married, she had many nieces and nephews to take to ball games every summer and hockey games in the winter.

It was one of those missed ball games

that led to a call to the Sheriff's Department about Mavis Bullard going missing. Her brother said that no one had been able to reach Mavis for two days, which was highly unusual. A request was made to have the department check her patio home. The deputy found her car at the house, but no Mavis. After determining that this was highly unusual, Mavis Bullard was added to the missing persons list, and the case was handed over to Deputy Haley and Special Agent Kolovich.

59

The heat of the Minnesota summer was in full force as the Missing Persons Team met the next morning. They added Mavis Bullard to their list and had everyone run checks. There was no use of Bullard's credit cards in the last three days, however Agent Fitzpatrick reported a call from a burner phone to Mavis Bullard just eight days prior.

Just to be sure, Haley sent a deputy out to check the gravesite in the marsh. In less than an hour the report came back with a picture showing no change at the site. It was beginning to look like the gravesite was a diversion created to get the Missing Persons Team to waste valuable time. "I hate being played, especially by a murderer," Haley said. "And it looks like he or she knows how to stay just a step ahead of us."

Mavis Bullard's body was discovered the

next morning, less than a half mile from where Jodi Karnetsky's remains were found. Kolovich and Haley arrived at the scene less than thirty minutes later. The first thing they both noticed was the marking on the forehead of the body. Two parallel lines which appeared to have been made with a marker.

While they waited for more information from forensics on the Bullard case, the team decided to again start from the beginning. Agent Fitzpatrick mused, "This sure isn't like those TV shows where the clues fit so neatly together and the identification of the criminal quickly becomes known." "We should be so lucky," said Haley, "Because if we were, the case would be solved by now.

60

Kolovich requested that Haley dispatch deputies to bring in Ireland and Dekich for an interview. Haley said he would not have either man handcuffed, and instructed a deputy to contact both men to ask that they stop at the Sheriff's office today. Greg Ireland would be coming in after lunch, but Dekich was out of town until tomorrow.

The farthest thing from Haley's mind right now was a date with Kolovich. He was extremely upset that she opted to bring in Ireland and Dekich. He told her so and indicated that he would sit in on each interview. "What purpose will this serve? I would stake my reputation on both of these guys." She replied, "I understand what you are saying, but I don't have your knowledge of the gentlemen in question, and I think we should shake the tree a little to be sure."

The interview with Greg Ireland went as Haley expected. Greg was forthcoming in all responses and noted that he called the Sheriff's Office on more than one occasion. About half way through the interview with Agent Kolovich, Ireland asked, "Am I being considered for something more that helping you guys out?" Haley responded before Kolovich could answer, telling Ireland that he didn't have any doubt about his involvement, or lack thereof. The look that Kolovich gave Haley was comparable to a laser.

"You should know that you never tell someone that they are not a suspect until you are absolutely sure." Kolovich was irate, and threatened to pull the case from local law enforcement. Haley answered in an even tone, "If you have any respect for me, and our department, now is the time to show it. I am telling you that there is no way that Ireland and Dekich are involved. Not even the little note and newspaper trick."

Haley continued, "When you first brought up their names, I had my department check out their alibis without their knowledge and found they both were elsewhere when a couple of the local abductions happened." "When were you going to share that bit of information with me?" asked Kolovich. "When you shared what you dug up, if anything, on your background search."

"Okay, I guess we both got a little bent out of shape here." Kolovich suggested having a drink and dinner to get things back on track. Despite still being upset, Haley agreed and they met later at Cabin Fever.

61

The next morning the team reviewed all information collected thus far in the missing person's cases, including the Bullard case. "It looks safe to assume that we are looking for a serial killer, at least in terms of numbers. We need to pull more information to find more commonalities between the victims, then use that to work backward to track our killer." After giving responsibilities to all team members, Kolovich decided to follow a hunch of her own.

That afternoon the team met and set their direction, planning to eliminate useless information and create a clearer picture of how each of the victims was connected. Special Agent Kolovich asked Margot Cosgrove to list information as it was given by team members. The evidence board showed Emily Vandenburg having grown up in St. Cloud, then leaving right after high school. She traveled first to Nashville, then Branson for only a short time before disappearing.

Dan Rutledge spent a good portion of his adult life in western Stearns County, and still resided there, except for the winter months spent in Texas. Other than shopping trips, there was no evidence that he spent any time in St. Cloud.

April Stevenson was born and raised in Wisconsin, went to college and began her career there as well. "Our only information on a connection to this area is a story she did about St. Cloud for her magazine. That was a couple of years ago. We need to get the exact dates and what she did while here."

Ray Strunk's entire life could be encapsulated by drawing a circle around Central Minnesota. He had never left the state, having traveled as far as Duluth to the north and the Twin Cities to the south. He told people that he had everything and everybody he needed in that area.

Jodi Karnetsky was born and raised in Central Minnesota, and attended college in the area before moving to Duluth for a new job. Although not reported to police, there was evidence that Jodi had been stalked while a student.

Willis Danvers grew up in Wisconsin and her only extended time in Minnesota was during college at Minnesota State in St. Cloud. Nothing noteworthy showed up in the file other than the reported stalker. "If the tie is here, why did she disappear in Wisconsin?" That question by Cosgrove went unanswered.

The latest victim, Mavis Bullard, had the Stearns County connection in every way. She had spent extended amounts of time in both ends of the county. The fact that she was a retired law enforcement officer was especially bothersome. Retired officers just weren't supposed to get murdered.

62

Special Agent Kolovich brought it all back together. "To get us going in a direction, we have to look at the St. Cloud connection. There are too many circumstances to point to random victims. Someone from around St. Cloud had to have made contact with each victim, either in St. Cloud or in the western part of the county. It's time to generate some ideas. Who was in a position to make contact with all the victims?"

Haley responded with, "If it weren't for Ray Strunk, I could see the following scenario. Someone spent their younger years, or worked, in the western end of the county. Then they moved to St. Cloud where they were in contact with younger people. It looks like someone made a list."

The ideas were bounced around,

including a student at Rutledge's school who lived in St. Mark. That could account for contacts with two of the older victims. As there were suggestions from eyewitnesses that the stalker was not a student at the college, the idea came up that he may have worked at the boat company and had come in contact with Ray Strunk there.

63

Haley and Kolovich headed out to St. Mark, to be followed by a visit to Rutledge's former school. The trip through rural Stearns County took them up Interstate 94, passing farmland and small towns along the way. At Melrose, they left the interstate and headed south.

St. Mark, a small town which had long ago lost its elementary school as students ended up going to bigger schools in the area. Though some of the school age youth went to Melrose, the majority went to Stearns County West. The school educated students from several area small towns, a few of which still had elementary schools.

It turned out that the St. Mark police department was comprised of a police chief and two part time officers. Current Chief, Delbert Hench, was a retired army master sergeant who took the job because the town couldn't find anyone else. Chief Hench happened to have retired to the family farm just outside of town and had some time on his hands, and few hobbies. Haley told Kolovich that this was a common occurrence in small towns with shrinking populations. It was either disband the police department and contract with the sheriff's department, or get by on the cheap.

They met Chief Hench in a small office in the rear of the small city hall. "Welcome to St. Mark, where old people drink coffee and young people move away." The chief was the composite of what the media determined long-time sergeants looked like. "I didn't even think the FBI knew we were here! What can I do for you?"

Haley explained the missing person cases, and the trail they were pursuing. He finished up with a question about old records and information about anyone harboring ill will against the past chief. "We have records, but they're in cardboard boxes stored in the garage out back. It wouldn't be a fun search with the cobwebs and dust. Regarding Chief Bullard, I can't help you. I never met her and have no knowledge of any issues she might have had. You might check with Verna up front, thought. She's been here since Nixon was in office."

64

After visiting with Verna Waldorf, Kolovich and Haley loaded up the old records with the promise of returning them in the same, or better, condition. "We can put Cosgrove to work on this mess, it will help show her the glamor of detective work. With Verna not aware of any threats or issues, the records are our only hope here." After grabbing lunch at Charlie's Café in Freeport, made famous by Garrison Keillor, they headed for the Stearns County West administration building with hopes of finding a thread to follow.

Stearns County West Superintendent Wesley Yellen had been on the job only two years, and did not know Dan Rutledge well, but had met him on a couple of occasions. He couldn't share much information about Rutledge, but was willing to help as much as privacy laws would allow regarding past students. As for information about Rutledge, Yellen told Kolovich and Haley that it was a case of a person waiting out his time to retire.   The staff and community had breathed a sigh of relief when Rutledge retired. Apparently he had made enough friends on the school board to hold on during the last few years.

Kolovich told Yellen what they wanted, and said that she would have a warrant faxed to him to cover sheltered information. They acquired the records of students who had been suspended or punished in some way by Rutledge during his 30 years. They also asked for a list of students at Stearns County West with a St. Mark address.   With the information, along with the boxes, Kolovich and Haley headed back to Haley's office.

65

The team began their investigation of the information gathered by Kolovich and Haley first thing the next day. Kolovich suggested creating a database of names from the school and the St. Mark records, then letting the computer spit out any names that showed up on both. It also would give them names to be run through a background check to see what might surface there.

Meanwhile, Haley had deputies serving warrants to get a list of employees at the boat factory who were employed the same time as Ray Strunk, and a list of high school classmates of Emily Vandenburg. And even though witnesses had said that the stalker at Minnesota State was not a student, a list of students at that time was also requested.

By early afternoon the lists had all been completed and cross referenced. There were 17 names of former students at Stearns County West who had worked with Ray Strunk. There were 56 names of former students who attended Minnesota State at the same time as the stalking incidents were reported. Of them, 26 were male. The report generated 119 names of persons who had a St. Mark address and attended Stearns County West while Rutledge was principal. A total of 38 former students received citations from Mavis Bullard during her term as Chief in St. Mark. There were a couple of "group charges" brought by Chief Bullard for skinny dipping at the lake at the edge of town. Chief Bullard had the reputation for confiscating all the clothes from the shore and having the kids find their way home. The Chief was always there to give rides as needed. There were no names attached to the group charges, but notes said it was kids from the area.

Four names showed up on the list four times, as former Stearns County West students, who had worked with Ray

Strunk, received citations from Chief Bullard, and were Minnesota State students. Special Agent Kolovich directed a complete background check on the four names, to include current contact information. Another 27 names appeared on three of the four lists, while 97 showed up on two of the lists.

Two department employees showed up on the lists, dispatcher Cliff Devlin and jailer Ralph Merrill. Both had worked with Ray Strunk after graduating from Stearns County West. Haley went to discreetly check for alibis in order to clear the department employees. Both had been in town at the time of the out-of-state abductions of Rutledge, Willis, Stevenson, and Vandenburg.

66

Kolovich and Haley focused on the names showing up four times on the lists. Taylor Wood, Mel Davenport, Ricky Nelstadt, and Josh Bellows all lived in the St. Cloud area. Armed with addresses and phone numbers, Haley and Kolovich left to do interviews with each of them. The rest of the team continued to try to eliminate names by other means.

Taylor Wood lived on the south side of St. Cloud and worked at the Crossroads Mall in the management offices. His name was quickly crossed off the list when it was determined that he had suffered a broken leg and had been wheelchair-bound for the last six weeks.

Mel Davenport, the sole female on the four person list, and Ricky Nelstadt were living together and working at home for a computer company out of Fargo. They had met at the boat company while attending college and were planning to marry in the fall. They had just returned from a trip to San Diego that put them out of the area when the last two abductions occurred. That left Josh Bellows as the last possibility to check out.

Josh Bellows lived in an old farmhouse a few miles northwest of the St. Cloud area. At one time the house had been ten miles from town, but the movement west after the big mall was built in the 60's started a growth spurt toward another one of the saints, St. Joseph. Everyone in Minnesota knew St. Joseph was the hometown of Jacob Wetterling, a young boy abducted by an unknown assailant in the late 80s. The case had never been solved.

Bellows worked as a groundskeeper at St. John's University, just a few miles past St. Joseph to the west. Kolovich and Haley found Bellows at home sitting on his deck with a beer in hand. "Sure I knew old Strunker, he was a perfect asshole. No brains, but had a little

authority and let it go to his head."
 Bellows said he had heard that Strunk had disappeared, but had not seen or talked to him in years. He had an alibi for the time period when Strunk disappeared which would need to be checked. Bellows concluded with a parting shot, "I would bet that no one is sorry that creep is gone."

67

Back at the task force meeting room, Kolovich and Haley shared the information about the visits with the four names from the list. "It sure looks like a dead end there, though we have to check out a couple of alibis." The day ended with assignments to check on the 27 names which had shown up three times. It didn't look like the process was going to get any easier.

With the weekend upon them, the task force members agreed to meet on Monday afternoon to compare notes and try to narrow the possibilities. Kolovich directed everyone to especially look for anyone who could not account for their whereabouts on the days of the abductions. She shared her fears with Haley that they would not have any strong suspects by Monday. "I wonder if we have someone else involved who is working with someone locally, or if it is

someone not on any of our lists." Haley responded, "I think that we have someone doing the abductions and someone else tweaking us locally.
 Whether the local person is just playing with us, or an active participant is yet to be seen."

68

Carmen Delaquez was growing tired of her shadow. She was uncomfortable going out with friends knowing that someone was watching her every move. She would not have been uncomfortable with her shadow if she had known that someone else was watching her and her shadow. Carmen decided that a little trip out without her shadow wouldn't be a problem as long as she stayed around people. She took some clothes and headed for the basement laundry room, telling her FBI friend that she was going to do some wash and wait for it to dry.

Once in the basement she slipped out a service door and was in her car in two minutes. It only took two more minutes to realize what a horrible mistake she had made. The hand over her face and the gun in her ear made her wish she was still doing her laundry. The last thing she remembered was a voice saying that the FBI wasn't all that smart.

69

Carmen woke up in a house with her hands and feet tied, and a cloth over her face. "Where am I? What do you want? Are you there?" Her questions were greeted with silence. It wasn't long before she heard a door close and the sound of footsteps coming closer.

"Are you quite comfortable my dear?" The voice was familiar. It was the voice on the phone. It was the voice of the guy who stalked her while she was in college. "Please, I don't have anything against you, I just didn't date in college," she cried.

"Let me tell you a story, I have high standards for success and never accept no for an answer. You see, it was inevitable that we'd have our date. Sad to say, I am currently having only one date per person. So, let's make it a good one, okay?" Carmen heard the sounds of papers being unwrapped and the sound of tape being pulled off a roll. She started to scream as the tape was put over her mouth.

70

The call from Special Agent Kolovich to Deputy Haley came about 8:45 on Sunday night. The worst had happened. Carmen Delaquez had been abducted despite having a security detail assigned to her. Though Carmen had slipped out on her own, the agent assigned was given a dressing down for not anticipating her actions. Though the agent had happened to see Carmen leaving the complex garage, he could not get to his car in time to follow.

"You see, I need to keep that task force on their toes. They're taking two steps forward and one step back.
 They're getting closer, but I'm almost done and then I'll disappear into life as usual and they will never catch me. If I could only trust you to keep your mouth shut, I would consider letting you live."

Carmen nodded her head aggressively in agreement. "Oh, you would keep quiet?
 Well, perhaps if you make this an evening to remember, we'll take that into consideration. You know, like a suspect who rats out a fellow crook to get a lighter sentence." Carmen nodded again.

Carmen's car was found about three miles from her apartment in a parking lot in Maple Grove. Efforts were already underway to check cameras in the area for a possible break. Forensic specialists were checking the car for any fingerprints or other evidence. "We should know more by the time we meet this afternoon. I sent word to everyone to check alibis for last night during any interviews this morning."   Haley told Kolovich he would see her later and set about checking a few things on his own.

The task force meeting opened with the news that two bits of information had come out about the abduction of Carmen Delaquez. Video surveillance showed that a light colored van had been parked in the lot when Carmen's car entered. Her car had pulled up next to the van. The side door of the van opened and something was moved from the car to

the van. The lighting in the back part of
the lot was not good, so no identification
of the person or the van's plates could be
made.

The second bit of information was that a
print was lifted from Carmen Delaquez'
car. That print was currently being run
through every database available. "If
our abductor has a record, or was in the
military, we should have something
within the hour. It may be a little longer
to run though everything else, but if he
is known, we'll find him." Agent Kolovich
then ran through the list of 27 names
given the past Friday.

Contacts had been made that morning to
twenty five of the twenty seven names,
with all having alibis for some or all of
the earlier abductions. And all but two
had concrete alibis for the previous
night. Haley added that he had checked
back and the original four names were all
clear as well. He continued, "I checked
on our graveyard this morning and there
were no changes. I also had deputies

check the area where the bodies of Karnetsky and Bullard were found. I hope to hear back from them at any time."

73

Carmen Delaquez was still alive. After her "date" last night she figured that she would be dead by now. She tried to think back to last night, however everything was blurry. It must have been something in the water or food he gave her. But she was alive, though still tied to a bed in a building of some kind. She tried to move but the restraints were too tight. She didn't know why she was still alive as her captor made it clear they were only having one date.

She again heard footsteps, knowing who as she could identify the walk by now. "Well, I bet someone could use another bathroom break." With that her feet were untied and she was led to the bathroom. "I am breaking with tradition and I think we're going to have another date tonight. Sound good to you?" Carmen, again tied to the bed and scared out of her wits, just nodded.

"Great! See you later."

74

"We have a name tied to the print in Carmen Delaquez' car. It comes back with the name Anthony LePatto. LePatto has a record for minor offenses in the Chicago area, and his last known address is in St. Louis, though that was three years ago. His parole officer in Chicago said LePatto was going into business with his brother-in-law. We have no more info, but have everybody looking for him." Kolovich then shared other information about efforts going on in an attempt to find the van through other cameras.

"Can you find out what kind of business LePatto's brother-in-law was in? Maybe it involves a van and we can get plate numbers to help in the search." Haley was about to continue when Devlin stuck his head into the task force room to report that the deputies found nothing in their search.

Agent Fitzpatrick posed the scenario, "Maybe this LePatto guy is just going around the upper Midwest abducting people for his own nefarious purposes and the ties to Central Minnesota are simply coincidences." Agent Norgaard countered with, "Heck, even the paperback detectives say that there is no such thing as a coincidence, but I don't see anything else working."

"I've decided that I really like you and, after our date tonight, I might let you go. But if I do, you can't tell anyone. Do you think you could do that?" Carmen nodded. "I'll decide after our date, which I'm sure will be even better than last night. Do you think so, too?" Another nod.

The next morning the task force started the day with an update, then directions for everyone to follow. Norgaard and Fitzpatrick were detailed to the LePatto search. Haley and Kolovich would oversee the review of the rest of the names garnered from their cross referencing. "If we're right, and the person responsible for these abductions is on our list, why are they doing this?" The question from Margot Cosgrove was answered, at the same time, by Haley and Kolovich. "Revenge." They had discussed this earlier over breakfast and felt it had to be some kind of payback.

"Our suspect must have created a bucket list of sorts, seeking vengeance against those who he, or she, feels wronged him at some point in the past. It works with Principal Rutledge if it were a former student. It works with Chief Bullard if it were for some charge that he feels was unwarranted. Everybody knows that Ray Strunk treated young people like trash and some of our young females' refusal to date him was seen as unfair." Haley added, "It fits together very well with the local connection. Our local guy hooks up with someone else to help in exacting his revenge. We think the parallel lines on the forehead of two of our victims is his way of saying, 'We are even now.'"

If LePatto was involved, as it seemed, how does a local person go to Chicago or St. Louis and hook up with a crook, Haley wondered out loud. "The Internet!" said Cosgrove. "Everything is on the Internet these days." One of the deputies asked, "What do you do, log onto dial-a-crook?" Haley agreed that the Internet was one option, and let Cosgrove run with it. He also asked Kolovich if the FBI could check the "Dark Net."

77

"Here's how it's going to work, I am going to show you some pictures. This is my safety net to assist you in keeping your word." Carmen could not see her captor as the room was dark and the only light was over her head. She was sitting in a chair in small room devoid of any other furniture that she could see, other than the bed.

"My parents, my nieces and nephews, why do you have them?" "I am going to let you go home tonight. I'm showing you these pictures so you know I have access to your family whenever I want. Do you want to keep them alive?"

Carmen, with tears in her eyes tentatively said, "Yes." "You will say nothing to anyone. You tell the cops and the FBI that you just needed to sneak away for a little while and now you are better. If you talk more than that, I will find out, and things will not go well for your family. Maybe little Emma will go first." The horror of the situation overwhelmed Carmen.

The news that Carmen Delaquez had returned to her apartment reached the FBI early the next morning. Haley and Kolovich were at her door in just under an hour.   After questioning her for a half hour and getting nowhere, a frustrated Haley said, "We know what you told us is not true. We know something else is going on here. We can't help if you don't give us something to work with."

 Carmen said, "I can't," and started to sob. Kolovich assigned a female special agent to stay with Carmen while she and Haley went for the breakfast they didn't have time for earlier.

Margot Cosgrove didn't tell Haley that she was more than a little familiar with the Internet. Computers started to interest her when she was given an iPad during elementary school. She had long ago decided that a career in law enforcement would require a deep knowledge of computers and the Internet.

Margot was very comfortable with finding lost, or hidden programs and deleted emails. She knew how to follow online traffic, and where to go for those things which the regular user didn't even dream of looking for. She just might have a way to point a finger at someone on the list based on what she could find.

Kolovich and Haley were back in the task force meeting room with the rest of the group, including on this occasion Sheriff Rafferty, before lunch. The discussion centered on Carmen Delaquez, and her abrupt reappearance. Carmen had been gone for thirty-six hours and wouldn't break from her story of "just getting away for a little while." She did consent to a medical checkup, but nothing more. The doctor had convinced Carmen to have blood drawn, with the results expected shortly.

Just before breaking for lunch, the results of the blood tests on Delaquez came in via email. Other than alcohol, evidence of the drug Rohypnol was found. "That may account for Carmen saying she couldn't help us, but I think there's more to it. We proved that she is not safe with us, so maybe she just sees no way out. I'm sending agents to interview family members to see if we can find a way to get her to open up."

The agent monitoring Carmen Delaquez called Kolovich just after lunch with the news that Carmen had received an email telling her that she was doing well, and that the person was looking forward to seeing her again. The message was signed, "Rafe". Kolovich immediately got agents on the email, trying to trace the sender. "It could be an innocent message, but the wording indicated knowledge of the past couple of days."

Word came shortly that the email had been sent from St. Cloud, originating from the Wi-Fi at the public library. "We are checking the public computers at the site, but anyone could log in, even from outside the library. If we're correct in assuming the email came from our suspect, then it solidifies the belief that he, or she, is local."

81

"Something that's been bothering me for a while now is the gravesite out at Beaver Falls. We've noted that our attention has been diverted several times when we started to focus on that area. Even when we went out there, someone was a step ahead of us, taunting us with that note and newspaper article." Haley stopped for a breath, but wasn't done. "I'm planning to go back out there to do a more thorough search, and in a wider area. We have people focusing on finding LePatto, we have people with Delaquez, and others are continuing to chase down names from our lists, so I think Beaver Falls needs another look see."

With Kolovich back in the Twin Cities hoping to get Carmen Delaquez to open up about the time she was gone, Haley took two deputies and got ready to head out to Beaver Falls. On the way out of the department, Devlin stopped them and asked Haley, "So, who's is in charge, with the Sheriff in DC and you guys heading out to Beaver?" "I am just a phone call away. For sure let me know if you hear from Agent Kolovich." Devlin thought he would like to hear from Agent Kolovich himself, but figured she was out of his league.

82

Devlin took his lunch and ate in the task force room, looking over the array of charts and lists on the abduction cases. He thought that maybe he should take some more classes and become a detective himself. Margot Cosgrove interrupted his reverie with a quick "Hi" as she came into the room. "You have all this stuff figured out?" asked Devlin. "No way, I just try to help out and stay out of the way. But once in a while I have an idea that they consider. We're making headways, but it is really slow. They think they have a line on the person doing the abductions, but can't find him." Devlin told her that he had to get back to his desk, but to let him know if she needed anything.

Margot Cosgrove was running checks of her own on every person on the list. The old saying that, "You'd be surprised by what is on the Internet about you," was true. She found some unflattering things about many of those on the task force list, though nothing so far that would incriminate anyone. But she was only getting started.

83

Special Agent Kolovich stopped at Carmen Delaquez' apartment to try again to get her to open up about her experience over the past weekend.
 Initially, Carmen refused to say anything except, "I can't." However, after Kolovich brought up Carmen's family, she broke down sobbing and said, "I don't know what to do. He said he would harm my family if I said anything to anyone. He said if I kept my mouth shut he would come by to pick me up for a date sometime soon. He said that maybe we could be friends."

Kolovich caught Haley just as he was leaving the department. She updated him on her conversation with Carmen Delaquez, and said the FBI had increased surveillance of all methods of communication to Delaquez. The FBI would also institute passive surveillance of her family. "I feel like the fabled donkey reaching for the carrot. It's out there, but I can't quite reach it." "Me, too," said Haley. "We're close, but are missing key evidence. This case has been like that from the beginning."

84

Anthony LePatto was hiding out in Kansas City, having learned that he had messed up in leaving a fingerprint in the Delaquez vehicle. All that trouble, and the dipstick had let the girl go. If he knew who the guy was, he might make a little visit to show his "appreciation." LePatto had never worked at a regular job in his life. Petty crimes as a teenager had let to armed robbery in his twenties. A seven-year hitch in prison led him to believe that he needed another career. A woman who had written to him in prison welcomed him into her life when he got out.

Rory Reynolds worked for a time as a computer programmer before branching out as an independent technology trouble shooter. That career change led her to contacts with some shady characters. At first, she was hesitant to get into the "dark side," as she called it, but the money was too good. She drove a BMW and had an upscale apartment in Minneapolis. Her "work" was done for clients throughout the Upper Midwest. She seldom traveled, and all financing was done online.

It was Rory's idea to set up a "procurement site" and she had pegged Anthony LePatto as her leg man. The site was set up to allow site users to request specific "items" to be secured and delivered, anonymously if desired. The price depended on the difficulty of securing the item, and the distance required to acquire and deliver the item. It had been a popular, and financially rewarding, endeavor. And until now, it had been flying below the radar.

As many of the requests involved something short of legal, Anthony leaving a fingerprint was a serious problem. From the beginning, as a precaution, all communications with Anthony had been in person or by burner phone. He had no idea how the requests were delivered to Rory. She felt that Anthony could be trusted to keep her involvement quiet if he was arrested, but with the severity of charges he might consider a plea. As a precaution, she shut down the site.

85

Haley and his deputies arrived at the location of the graves later that morning. "I want to check out the entire area in a methodical fashion. We will start out twenty-five feet from the center of the graves and mark anything unusual out as far as one hundred and fifty feet if possible. We'll also want to search along either side of the path coming into this area." After assigning sectors for each of them, the search began.

The terrain was extremely difficult at times to travel. It was spotted with bogs, low bushes, and matted grasses. The officers had brought along plastic poles with numbered flags attached. Any possible evidence was marked and noted. After three hours, the officers met at the graves and compared notes. As it turned out, seven flags had been placed in the swamp around the graves. Clothing, a broken shovel, and an empty purse were three items of special interest.

Haley explained the next step of the search. "We now get to the hard part of our search. In the past when we came out here it seemed like this was just some kind of game for someone playing with us. It looked like a Halloween display. But what we found today probably indicates that there's more here than we have found so far." Haley then had the men fill in the empty graves while he recorded observations on his phone.

86

Kolovich arrived at the Beaver Falls "graveyard" just as the men were finishing putting the dirt back in the original holes. "I came out because something occurred to me that we may have been missing."

Haley responded, "Like what might be under the piles of dirt that we figured had just been piled next to the empty graves? You had the same thought, didn't you?" Kolovich followed the thought, "Every time we came out here or discussed the site I felt that there was something that we just couldn't see."

Haley agreed, "I feel kind of stupid not thinking about this before. And, we may be wrong, but I think we fell for a slight of hand – or slight of dirt as the case may be."

When the empty graves had all been

filled in, Haley took a shovel and went to the site of the first grave and started turning over dirt from where the pile had been. It didn't take long to find a body under only a foot of dirt. While Kolovich left to summon forensics and a recovery team, Haley went to the second grave and in short order discovered a second body.

"It's irritating that even though we figured that the "graveyard" site was significant, it took us this long to figure it out." "Well, in our defense, our killer played us pretty well, leading us off in another direction whenever we got close," answered Kolovich. "Which makes me wonder how he, or she, was able to play us so well." They both were thinking the same thing: someone had to know what they were doing soon after they made plans. "Someone in one of our departments?"

87

Margot Cosgrove was finding out a lot of information about people on the suspect list, but still had not found a connection to any of the victims, other than coincidental contact. The two department people, Cliff Devlin and jailer Ralph Merrill, were in the clear, based on her research thus far. Either someone on the list was really good at covering their tracks, or their perpetrator was not on the list. She had to dig deeper.

It took an entire day to recover the bodies, five of them, from the graves at Beaver Falls. Though positive identification had not been made, it was fairly clear that the bodies were of their missing persons, April Stevenson, Dan Rutledge, Emily Vandenburg, Ray Strunk, and Willis Danvers. It would take some time for the autopsies and for forensic evidence to be processed.

Some preliminary results were available the following day, including the notation that each of the victims had the equal sign inked on the forehead, and indications were that the victims had each been strangled. The task force now knew for sure that they were pursuing a serial killer.

88

The next day brought the team together in the task force room, trying to put their finger on the one thing that would break the case. "I think we've made a lot of progress, but need that string to tie it all together. Any ideas?" Kolovich continued, "We're fairly certain that Anthony LePatto is involved in at least one of the abductions. There is also ample evidence that he has a local partner." Agent Fitzpatrick noted that LePatto had been tracked to Kansas City, though was not currently in custody.

Haley suggested going back through the list of "potential" suspects. "Let's assume that our local guy or gal had interaction with Dan Rutledge during high school, may have been busted by Chief Bullard, and worked with Ray Strunk. We have no idea if our perp went to the college, or just hung around. Then we go back through each of them to check alibis and see if anything pops up in regard to unusual behavior. We need to find out if any of them traveled out of the area at any time, or had opportunities to connect with LePatto."

Kolovich decided to key into anyone on the list who may have had opportunity to hold Carmen Delaquez, and to bring her back to the Twin Cities. "I am going to interview Carmen again to see if I can get her to remember anything about the place she was held captive. Maybe she'll remember something about the trip back to her apartment."

Cosgrove got approval to continue computer searches on a local basis, assuming correctly that the FBI had completed searches on a mass scale. Fitzpatrick and Norgaard would fly to Kansas City to take over the search for LePatto. Deputies were assigned to recheck alibis, and interview any associated persons who may not have been available during the original cursory search.

89

Greg Ireland and Nick Dekich were active in the Upper Mississippi Orienteering Club. The group set up challenges for members and invited guests to learn more about the sport and to try their hand at traversing the course. They went out to Beaver Falls to set up a course for the following weekend, to be held in conjunction with Lumberjack Days in the small town of Leader.

Beaver Falls was a great place for the Orienteering course. Though it had rolling hills and lowlands, it was not a difficult course for those new to the sport. As they set the locations on the course, they came to the area where Greg had first heard the noise that led him to call Chief Deputy Haley. "That little rise out in the march would be a great location, but I think that Haley would shoot us if we even got close to that area. Let's get the last checkpoint set so we can get everything finalized tonight at the meeting."

Just as Haley was about to leave the office for the day, Cliff Devlin stuck his head in the task force room and told him about the strange phone call he had just received. "The caller said that two people were out at the strange cemetery where you found the bodies. The voice was muffled, but also indicated that they were carrying what looked like sticks or shovels. He wouldn't give a name, but he thought you should know about it. A number showed up on caller ID, but it must be from a burner phone as there was no name attached."

Carmen Delaquez was not able to give Agent Kolovich much more information about where she was held. She thought it was a house or apartment, not a shed or other outbuilding. Though she was drugged or blindfolded for a majority of the time, she remembered that the place kind of echoed, like it was mostly empty. As for her trip back to her apartment from where she had been held, she could not help.

She remembered waking up in the vehicle when she was poked by her captor and told she should get out and walk the two blocks to her apartment. She was told not to look back or she would be shot. Carmen thought the vehicle was a SUV. She remembered seeing red duct tape on the door panel in the back seat, and thought the SUV was a dark color.

Fitzpatrick and Norgaard arrived in Kansas City and met the local police at the FBI Regional Center. According to a reliable informant, LePatto had been staying with some people above a bar in the south side of the city. Bud's Suds was not part of the upscale bar scene in KC, nor was the neighborhood a go to place for anything but drugs and prostitution. An undercover team had been watching the apartment, but had seen no sign of LePatto. "Let's station some officers in back to cover the fire escape, and we'll go knock on the door," offered Fitzpatrick.

When everybody was set, Fitzpatrick and Norgaard went up the stairwell along the side of the old bar, listening carefully for sounds from above. At the landing they took positions on each side of the door and knocked on the door. As Norgaard was about to knock again, they heard the security chain rattle and the door open a couple of inches. "What do you want?" came the question from a woman who looked to be fifty years old, but may have only been in her thirties. She had the look of someone who had gotten up on the wrong side of the bed every day of her life.

"FBI ma'am, may we come in? "Just give me a couple of minutes to put something on." Fitzpatrick and Norgaard heard voices, then a slammed door.
 Before the woman came back, the agents heard through the earpiece that one Anthony LePatto had been apprehended coming down the fire escape. Both the woman and LePatto were taken to FBI headquarters for questioning. At first LePatto denied having been in the Twin Cities recently, but changed his story when the agents told him of reliable witnesses putting him there.

93

The task force met the next morning at 7:30 and learned of the apprehension of Anthony LePatto in Kansas City. LePatto had said that he was in the Twin Cities and, to explain his fingerprints in Carmen Delaquez' car, he said that he broke into several cars looking to steal one for the trip to Kansas City. He would not admit to knowing anything about Delaquez, or her car. He was being held in Kansas City on possible auto theft charges. Haley told the task force about the anonymous phone call at the end of the previous day. He said that he had dispatched deputies to the area, but no one was found.

94

He figured that he had completed his list of seven, but couldn't resist pointing the finger at Ireland and Dekich. He thought that the task force should have a little excitement for a day or so on that false lead. The beauty of it was that he had given them an additional tip beyond the phone call. An eighth grave was added to the seven that officers had found before. Although he was done, you just never know when you might have need for another grave. Now he would just wait until someone noticed it.

95

Margot Cosgrove's research – it was really hacking – led her to search for local properties which were vacant. She found several in the area near where the seven graves were located, and close to where two of the bodies were found.
 She listed the properties and owners on the white board in the task force room and decided to go look at a few of the properties that were within 15 miles.
 She started with a property down the road from Eunice Daggett.

The first thing Margot noted were fresh tire tracks in the yard which led to an old barn that had once been painted red, but was now a rusty gray in color. Although the barn was in poor condition, it had a lock on the front double doors. She walked around to the side and found that another door was also bolted shut. The few windows were way too murky to see through, and Margo decided that breaking a window was not an option. She walked over to the old farmhouse and was able to go in through the front door. Broken glass littered the floor and a few pieces of old furniture were obviously used for animal habitat. There was dust on everything and it was very obvious that no one had spent time in the house for a long time.

96

Haley arrived back at task force headquarters at mid-morning to get ready for the daily update. He noted Cosgrove's addition to the evidence board with a smile. That young lady will make a good detective one day, he thought. He knew it was a long shot, but that kind of detail work might help at some point. He knew some of the property owners, and a few of the others sounded familiar. At some point he hoped to have a couple of deputies freed up to check out the locations. Until then, he would have Kolovich run each of the names through FBI files to see if anything of interest came up.

Special Agent Kolovich and the other agents and deputies arrived for the daily briefing and to determine assignments for the day. After a quick review of investigations from the day before and that morning, Haley noted the information listed regarding vacant properties. "Margot left a note saying she might not be in today, but she did some research on vacant properties that may help. But without a specific area to search, it is a long shot at best."

 Kolovich listed seven names which had question marks from the review of potentials from the original suspect list.

 "These seven had some question marks, even though our first interviews seemed to clear them.   Let's give them a more thorough investigation to see if there are any holes, or to give them the all clear."

97

Cosgrove decided to go back to the barn to look for another way to see what was behind the locked doors. She stepped through an old wooden rail fence and went around the back. She was in the old barnyard and the weeds and brush made it hard to move along the side. She almost fell into a trench and remembered that a lot of farms had barn cleaners which automatically moved manure and old bedding out. She blocked that thought from her mind and stooped low to crawl through the two foot high opening.

Once inside the barn she saw a couple of pieces of farm equipment, some hay, and an old car. A closer look showed that none of the pieces of equipment, nor the car, had been disturbed recently.
 Near the front locked door was a small door leading to side room in the front corner of the barn. The door creaked as

Margot opened it, and inside the room she found what looked like a laboratory. She mused, I think I stumbled upon a drug operation. Great detective I am, she thought, I'm in here and don't have a warrant. She scooted out the back opening and headed through the weeds to her car.

98

Haley was in the task force room by himself after the others left to pursue the investigations assigned. Kolovich was making phone calls, with the plan to be back shortly. Looking at the list provided by Cosgrove, he wondered why she had listed all the properties, but then had erased two of them. Not a big deal, but why write them down, only to erase them? When Agent Kolovich returned, she and Haley decided to catch an early lunch at the Fort, a rustic bar and restaurant in Fort Ripley, then do another walk through the graveyard at Beaver Falls.

They contacted the DNR and made arrangements to have an officer meet them with an ATV for the ride in to save time. On the way in the DNR Officer noted a couple of the sites set up for the orienteering challenge coming up on the weekend. "I think that explains the two guys with 'shovels' in the report we got."

The new grave was both surprising and upsetting. "Just like before, either someone has a sick sense of humor, or we are being played again," said Haley. They checked the area thoroughly, including looking under the pile of dirt, and found nothing that indicated any foul play. "We haven't had any new reports locally about missing persons. Maybe you could get the FBI wheels checking nationally to see if any fit our guidelines."

99

The temp officer running dispatch had a message for Haley when he and Kolovich returned to the department. "Eunice Daggett called and said that she and Reginald were out for a walk and saw a couple of cars go into the old Davenport farm. She said that she rarely sees cars go there, and that two in one day was suspicious." Haley explained who Eunice and Reginald were, and that she was, by herself, the neighborhood watch. Haley had dispatch send a car out to check out the property. "We can kill two birds with one stone here, the Davenport place is on Cosgrove's list."

One by one, the seven names of interest on Kolovich's list were cleared, with only two left to clear. About thirty minutes later, the report came in from the Davenport farm. Nothing out of place, no evidence of damage other than by

Mother Nature, but a car was found with no one around. The car was a Pontiac Sunbird, registered to a Colleen Rutherford of Melrose, a town about 30 miles from St. Cloud. "I wonder if she is related to Commissioner Rutherford, Margot Cosgrove's uncle," thought Haley. "Wait, I think that is the car Margot drives," said one of the deputies.

Margot came around the corner of the barn, slipped through the rail fence and noticed another car parked by the house. "Hello, I'm Margot Cosgrove from the Sheriff's Department." She received no response. She looked and saw that the lock was still on the front door of the barn. Maybe someone was looking to buy the property and was out looking it over.

The car looked familiar, but she couldn't remember where she had seen it. As she turned to get into her car, she saw someone in the other car waving at her. As she walked up to the car, she recognized the person inside. She also recognized the gun pointed at her.

On the way to the Davenport farm, Haley radioed for confirmation that the owner of the car was Margot's mother. By the time they completed the 15 minute drive, they had that confirmation. It was indeed, Margot's car. After checking the house and immediate area, and getting no response to shouts, Haley ordered the forensics team out to the farm. One of the deputies noted that someone had gone around the back of the barn and called Haley over. After seeing that someone had entered through the small back door, Kolovich agreed that probable cause allowed them to cut the lock at the front. Haley stationed the deputy at the back, and another at the side door, then cut the lock and entered with Kolovich.

Other than finding the drug paraphernalia and the equipment and car, the barn was empty. The forensics team was going through Cosgrove's car and making castings of the tire marks.

"I hope there's a reasonable explanation for Margot's car being here without her, but I doubt it. It may be that she saw the drug setup and was caught doing so, but it might be connected to the list she put together." There was no indication that Carmen Delaquez had been held here, and nothing else to tie the farm to any of the deaths.

102

"Are you manufacturing drugs, is that why you kidnapped me?" Margot felt that she could talk her way out of anything, and the fact that she knew her assailant made her confident.

"You're an amusing little thing, but you would have made a poor detective. Do you think that you're the first person to be tied to that bed? Does the name Carmen Delaquez ring a bell with you?" Margot's confidence took a huge hit as she realized that she had found the serial killer that they had been tracking.

"I'm afraid that your nosiness has cost you dearly. I was done with my list. I had taken care of each of the bastards who helped ruin my life. Mr. Rutledge was nothing but a dumb ex-jock, and that police chief thought she could get by with parading me naked in front of everybody. Those college girls won't get to be snobbish to anyone else now, will they?   And let's not forget old Strunker. He was a perfect example of a waste of oxygen. Ordering us around even though his shoe size was higher than his IQ!"

Margot looked around and wondered where on the property she was. "Agent Kolovich and Deputy Haley will figure out your connection to this place and hunt you down." Margot's hope was quickly shattered.   "Another little mistake on your part. I have no connection to the Davenport farm, you're at my little hideaway now. During your little nap that I helped you with, we took a drive. And guess what, this place was on your list, but I erased it. So they can check all the others and won't find mine."

When her kidnapper left, Margot tried to get free, but was handcuffed to the bed. She started to sob when she realized what was likely to happen, unless Kolovich and Haley were able to solve her disappearance—-and quickly. She thought about her mother, and how sad she would be. She looked around the room in which she found herself. She had to focus on a way to get away – it was going to be up to her.

103

"We need to find Margot. The list she made, the eighth grave, her disappearance, it's all tied together. We find Margot, we find our killer. I just hope it's not too late. We need to check on each of the places on the list. What about the last two names on your list?"

Kolovich told the group that the last two names from the list not cleared were the two department employees, Cliff Devlin and Ralph Merrill. Since Devlin was off at the St. Cloud Hospital with his uncle, Kolovich and Haley had Merrill meet them in the task force room. If he was involved, they thought bringing him in the room would make him nervous, perhaps nervous enough to confess. But Merrill didn't confess, and had a solid alibi for when Carmen Delaquez had been held hostage somewhere in the area.

Merrill saw the lists of properties listed on the board. "I guess you cleared Cliff Devlin's grandpa's place. I see you erased it." The magic marker could still be seen in a shadowy form. "He told me several times about inheriting the property up outside of Cushing. He liked how peaceful it was up there. That when he was sheriff he would build a big house up there." As soon as Merrill was out the door, Haley put in a call to the St. Cloud Hospital to see if they could find Cliff Devlin. "I think Ralph might have put us onto something. If we don't find any uncle of Devlin's at the hospital, we might just have found our killer."

While Merrill was being interviewed, Cliff Devlin had called dispatch and said his uncle was better, but that he was taking the next couple days off for a short vacation. He said he would be camping up north, therefore would not be accessible by phone.

As soon as Haley completed his call to the hospital, he and Kolovich were headed for Devlin's property. They waited for the requested backup a half mile from the Devlin property under an old forest service tower. Looking at their GPS, they noted that there was only one road into the property, however, a forest service dirt track went out the back of the property. Kolovich and Haley would take the front, with the backup officers covering the back by way of the forest service road.

104

"Well Margot, we have a long weekend to get acquainted. Unfortunately, only one of us will be going back to work on Monday. As you know, there are many wild animals up here in the woods. Coyotes, wolves, and even some black bears are in the area. Everybody will think you went camping and ran into some problems."

"You won't get away with it," Margot yelled.

"Oh, but I will. I am going to move your car tonight and leave a note that you went camping. Everybody knows what an outdoor lover you are." Margot struggled with the restraints. "Would you like to join the "87 Club with me before your camping experience? I know you said you weren't going to date anyone from the department until after your internship, but now that we know it is over…"

Margot woke up from the drug given to her by her attacker. She was staked to the ground in a grassy area with trees on all sides. Her clothes were in tatters, having been cut off. Besides the bugs and ants, she saw nothing. The birds were chirping happily, and she saw an eagle soaring high above. She heard footsteps coming through the grass behind her head. Then, Cliff Devlin stepped into view carrying a chunk of raw meat. "Kind of like my little invite to the carnivores later, after our little date. Sorry, but you and I are only going to have one date. My friend Carmen and I will have more dates. She was willing to party with me, and will again. Sadly for you, I only need one girlfriend."

After getting word that the deputies were in place at the rear of the property, Kolovich and Haley drove up to the cabin on Devlin's land. They came in from either side to approach the front door of the cabin, careful to stay away from the one window. After knocking and getting no response, Haley tried the knob and the door slowly opened. Inside was one large room with a door off the side that probably was a bath. In the far left corner was a bed with handcuffs still attached to the bedposts. A purse and a set of keys was on a small table next to the bed. Kolovich opened the purse and found a license and two credit cards, all in the name of Margot Cosgrove. Haley cleared the bathroom and radioed the deputies to come in from the back.

Devlin pulled out a colorful silk scarf and tied it loosely around Margot's neck. She tried to spit in his face and screamed. He hit her across the ear and tied the scarf tighter. "It looks like good old duct tape is in order. I find that things are quieter and I don't get bitten during the date. So, are we doing this together, or do I tie the scarf tighter to get a reaction from you?"

Just as Haley stepped out the door of the cabin, he heard a faint scream. Calling Kolovich and the deputies, they headed in the direction of the scream, following a faint path into the woods. After about a quarter mile, they saw movement in a clearing about a hundred yards ahead. Spreading out, they crept closer until they could see someone kneeling over a person on the ground.

Just then, one of the deputies stepped on a branch that cracked loudly. Devlin spun around, gun in hand, looking for the cause of the noise. Haley stepped into the clearing about fifty feet from Devlin. "Cliff, it's over." Kolovich and the two deputies came into view equally spread out on either side of Kolovich and Haley. Devlin pointed the gun at Cosgrove's head, "I'll kill her if you don't drop your guns right now."

As Haley stepped forward, he said, "That's not going to happen. I am coming up to you and you will give me your gun. If you shoot me, my backup will drop you in a matter of seconds." Haley kept walking, his gun pointed at Devlin. "No! I was going to get away with this. If she hadn't made that list, I would have pulled it off." Devlin took the gun from Cosgrove's head and pointed it at his own.

108

The next day, as the task force wound down, Cosgrove related how Devlin had told her about the supposed atrocities committed against him by the victims. She also related how Devlin had thought he was going to get away with it, including her murder. Devlin had told her how he had found the "procurement" website, knowing that he had found a way to get even with those people who had wronged him.

Though Cliff Devlin was a kidnapper, rapist and murderer, he broke down rather than pull the trigger. He would spend the rest of his life in prison. Rory Reynolds couldn't wait to finger Devlin and LePatto when the FBI showed up at her door. And it did not take long for LePatto to try to trade years for info on the other two. In the end, it did not help. Both would spend the majority of the rest of their lives in prison as well.

Special Agent Kolovich and Chief Deputy Haley kept their date by going camping at Crow Wing State Park on the banks of the Mississippi River. They camped near where the Red River ox carts crossed long ago. However, their accommodations were much more modern, and the fishing was good.

Watch for the next Kolovich and Haley case.

Please review this book at Amazon.com